# SHORT STORIES COLLECTION VOL.1

## JOHN MOORE

authorHOUSE®

*AuthorHouse™ UK Ltd.*
*1663 Liberty Drive*
*Bloomington, IN 47403 USA*
*www.authorhouse.co.uk*
*Phone: 0800.197.4150*

*Published by AuthorHouse 05/16/2014*

*ISBN: 978-1-4969-8128-8 (sc)*
*ISBN: 978-1-4969-8129-5 (hc)*
*ISBN: 978-1-4969-8130-1 (e)*

# Global rescue—
# Blackpool Disaster

# Chapter 1

⟫‑◦‑⟪

G lobal Rescue has been operational for a year and a half now, and they have done 30 rescue's to date. Not a lot I hear you say, but they don't go to a rescue they know the local rescue services can handle, unless they are asked to join in.

Blackpool is one of the most thought of destination for a holiday, and the top spot to visit is the pleasure beach. Here holiday makers and tourists can enjoy the rides and fun that Blackpool has to offer.

The ride most people go to 1st is the rollercoaster ride called "The Big One", and this coaster has the steepest first downhill section in the world. The coaster stands 235ft at its highest point, and it reaches speeds upto 74mph. Thrill seekers love the G forces this ride has to offer and it's a very popular ride here.

The pleasure beach has lots of rides and places of entertainment for the whole family. Of course Blackpool tower is another main attraction along with the sea front amusements.

It's now summer in Blackpool, but this year has been an unusually wet one, but this hasn't deterred the crowds enjoying the sights and sounds. The weather never deters the people here, but the past week the rain has been heavy and constant, but now it has stopped and the sun is out.

People line up to go on the Big one coaster and they all get excited as the next set of 6 cars pull into the boarding area. Each car can hold 6 adults with ease. The next set of coaster passengers climb into the cars, and they sit down and the safety bar is lowered.

The ride begins and they all look at the long climb to the top and it impressive to see, and the men, women and children get excited now. Halfway up the climb the track and structure begins to shake, but they all think this is normal.

Behind one of the many burger bars a small hole has appeared but no one has noticed it yet. The hole is due to the vast amount of rain that has fallen in the past week, and the sub soil has been eroded away under the burger bar.

Back on the coaster the cars are now getting close to the top. One of the men on the front car looks around to see if they can find any reason for the structure shaking, then he looks down and spots the hole. It's about 300yds from the coasters main structure, and he points it out to the rest of them.

"Look at that" he says pointing to the hole. His wife looks at him.

"Look at what dear?" she says, smiling at him.

"Look, it's a hole" he says again, "why is there a hole there?"

A woman close behind them looks over to see the hole, now getting bigger as they watch. "My god it's getting bigger. Should it be doing that?"

"I don't think so" the man says to her. "Something isn't right here." Then the ride shakes again and this time it lasts longer, and is more violent. The cars begin to shake and rattle as they climb up the slope, and the passengers are nervous now, so they scream out.

Down on the ground the crowds hear them scream but they think it's just because of the ride. Some people look up and then a woman sees the track moving.

"Look at that, the track is swaying" she says to her friends, "is it supposed to be doing that?"

Her friend looks up and sees the track moving. "I don't think it's meant to do that." She looks at her friend, a worried look on her face. "We'd better tell someone."

Near the burger bar the hole has now grown and is around 20ft in diameter, and the owner of the bar comes out to empty some rubbish, and he spots it. He runs back into his burger bar to get the people out, but before he can say anything there is a loud rumbling sound and the ground begins to shake.

Outside they can hear people shouting and screaming, and the people in the bar get up and run to the doors, but the ground collapses beneath them, and in a midst of screams, dust and falling debris, the burger bar disappears down the hole.

All around the area people are running and screaming to get out of the way, but most of them fall into the opening hole.

On the Big One rollercoaster the cars have reached the top and are now beginning the steep drop, then the track begins to sway and buckle, and as the cars pick up a bit of speed the passengers hope they can get down the steep slope.

The cars sway even more and suddenly the track buckles severely and the 6 cars come to an abrupt stop, and one man is thrown out of the 2$^{nd}$ car back from the front. He falls to the ground as onlookers look on in horror. He hits the ground with a thud, and his body explodes from the impact, and people scream in horror.

The 6 cars are now jammed halfway down the steep slope and the other passengers are screaming in fear. The track has buckled and jammed the cars. Then as people on the ground look up at them the track and structure 20ft from the cars collapses into the sinkhole.

The sinkhole is now 300ft in diameter and 70ft deep, and rides, people and shops have been sucked down the hole. Around the edge of the sinkhole a crowd of people have gathered and some look over the edge to see if they can see anyone.

They can hear people screaming and they shout out to them, just to let them know someone can hear them. In the distance everyone can hear the sirens of the local rescue services speeding to the disaster area.

A news reporter who has been interviewing the holiday makers and tourists sees the commotion and she and her crew go over to the sinkhole, and they can't believe what they are seeing. The woman and her crew begin to report on the sinkhole and they interview a lot of people to get their stories of what happened.

The news report goes out all over the country and in their homes people watch in horror as they hear the stories from the people there. The woman reporter gets her camera man to show the people in the stranded cars on the Big One's rollercoaster. All around the country people watching the news report can see these poor and frightened passengers stuck in the cars, 20ft from a sheer drop into the sinkhole.

The news reporter is in tears as she reports what she can see and hear, and all over the UK people watch as they show the devastation caused by this unusual sinkhole.

The rescue services arrive at the scene and they spread out along the sea front near the pleasure beach park. One fireman spots the news reporter and her crew and he goes over to her.

"What's the situation here? Have you been filming this for the TV?"

"I have been filming it and it is going out live as we speak all over the country. I have no idea what is going on and what caused this hole to appear, but one thing I do know is that those people" and she points to the passengers trapped on the rollercoaster, "are in serious trouble." The reporter looks at the fireman and smiles.

He looks up and sees the coaster cars. "Good god" he says, looking alarmed. "I'll get the chief." The fireman goes back to the fire tender and he calls his chief over. "Chief, can I see you sir?"

The chief comes over. "What's up Jerry?"

"Take a look up there chief" he says to him as he points to the trapped passengers.

He looks up. "My god" he says then all the other fire crews come over. "OK you lot, anyone got any ideas on how we can get them down from up there?" he looks at the crews and they all look up at the coaster cars stuck halfway down the steepest slope on the ride.

"Well it's too risky using a ladder chief. The ladder may cause the structure to shake and they could all fall into the hole." The fireman says and everyone agrees.

"It looks like we are going to need help on this one. We can help all those trapped at the bottom of this sinkhole, but these people need professional help. Anyone got any ideas?" The chief looks at his crews.

# Chapter 2

At Global Rescue's base the team in the command room monitor all communications from radio, C.B. and television and one of the operative's spots the news report from Blackpool. She calls Dave (the owner) to the command room and when he gets there they watch the news report from earlier.

Jenny Wilson, Dave's comms operator on the crane/ladder truck, goes over to him and stands by his side.

"Are we going to help Dave?" she asks, still looking at the news report.

"I think the local rescue services can handle this one Jenny. Let's keep the link and all emergency frequencies open, just in case." He looks at Jenny and she nods in agreement.

Back at Blackpool the rescue services are now putting plans into operation to get the people out of the 70ft deep sinkhole, but the fire crew from tender 4 are trying to think of a way to rescue the stranded and frightened people in the coaster cars. The chief gathers his crew.

"So has anyone got any ideas on how to get them off that structure?" The chief waits for any suggestions.

"No idea chief, this is a tricky one, even for us chief." One of them says and the others agree with him.

"Well we need some sort of plan you lot, any idea will do."

"With respect chief, I think this one is out of our expertise. We need someone who has specialised equipment to get them off that twisted structure. It will be very dangerous chief."

The chief looks at them. "So who can we get for this dangerous job?

"To my knowledge there is only one service to call, and that's Global Rescue." All the crew turn and look at him. The chief goes over to him.

"Global Rescue, of course. Why didn't I think of that? Well done Jerry." The chief goes over to the fire tender, climbs in and picks up the mic. "This is chief John Laws of fire tender 4, calling Global Rescue, come in please."

The rest of his crew go over to the fire tender and listen in. There is no answer, so he repeats the call. "This is chief John Laws of fire tender 4 calling from Blackpool pleasure beach, calling Global Rescue, come in please." They all listen in and then to their relief a reply comes back.

"This is Global Rescue to chief John Laws, how can we help?" Dave has replied to them all.

"Thank heavens" he says happily, "we have a bad situation here at Blackpool pleasure beach, sir."

"We have been monitoring the news reports chief. Not a nice situation there eh chief, and please call me Dave."

"It certainly isn't a good situation Dave. We can handle the people down the sinkhole, but we would like you to see what you can do for those passengers trapped on the Big One rollercoaster."

"We have seen their situation chief, and it doesn't look too good."

"So can you help Dave?" the chief and his crew listen intensely for the answer.

"Of course we can chief. Now what is the situation at this moment in time?" Dave needs to know all the info.

"As we can see from here Dave the passengers are stuck halfway down the steep slope, but the track about 20ft away, has collapsed and it's only the twisted and buckled track that is holding them there."

"How does the structure look chief?"

"It looks ok at the moment, but we didn't want to risk climbing up or using a ladder in case it shook the structure."

"Wise move chief. Ok we are on our way. Just keep an eye on those passengers and try to reassure them, and let them know help is on its way. We will be there within the hour chief."

"Ok Dave, we'll do what you say, and please hurry because I think it may collapse if the sinkhole gets bigger." His voice sounds nervous, but Dave is totally calm.

"Don't panic chief we are on our way, over and out." The chief looks at his crew and tells them what to do, and they put up a cordon barrier around the open hole near the rollercoaster. When the cordon has been put up a crowd gathers around it and the fire crew make sure no one gets too close.

At Global Rescue's base Dave gets everyone in the command room, and when they are all there, he stands in the centre of the huge room.

"Ok everyone we have to get to Blackpool as quickly as we can. Neil you inform the motorway police patrols on the M6 to clear us a path. Angela, you keep in touch with the fire chief and his crew at the scene and pass all reports to me, ok?"

"Yes Dave" Angela replies.

"Ok we will need the crane/ladder truck, 2 super ambulances, 2 road cruisers and 2 airborne grapple jets." He looks round the room and everyone is excited, but some of them know they won't be going, but they still have a part to play. "Ok lets go, time is critical for those passengers on those coaster cars."

Dave and his crane/ladder crew run out to their truck, along with the crews of the other vehicles and the 2 grapple jets. The road cruiser crews are the first to leave because they go ahead to warn others that Global Rescue are on their way.

The full rescue team leave the base, only 10 minutes after the meeting, and head for the M6, which will take them to Blackpool.

The convoy of vehicles look impressive as they speed down the M6, in the outside lane. People in cars, lorries or on coaches watch as these huge rescue vehicles scream past them. The biggest vehicle in the convoy is the 129.6ft long, 10ft wide crane/ladder truck and most people love this truck, especially children. As they pass cars and coaches with children on the kids always look out the windows to get a look at this huge truck.

Halfway down the M6 2 police officers are warning vehicles to stay out of the outside lane, when the new officer spots the 2 road cruisers closing fast. He turns to his experienced colleague.

"Look at these" he says pointing to the road cruisers. "Is this them?"

Officer Branton has seen Global Rescue many times before and he knows what it's like to see these unusually large vehicles for the first time. "Yep this is them, but they are only the lead vehicles" and he looks at his new officer, who looks slightly puzzled, "you ain't seen nothing yet, just wait."

They both keep watching then in the distance they see the red and orange Hi Glo flashing lights on the crane/ladder truck as it approaches. The sirens are so loud, you can hear them half a mile away, and they can now see the crane/ladder truck, with its distinctive deep yellow paintwork and green stripe and a world globe with a red band around it, on a 45 degree angle. All the vehicles have this paintwork, stripe and world globe on them.

As the truck passes the 2 officers, the new recruit watches in awe, and then the other vehicles pass them and he can't believe their sizes. He has seen them on the TV but never up close. "God they are amazing, especially that crane/ladder truck" he says watching them in the distance, "I never knew they were so big."

# Chapter 3

————◆————

Blackpool traffic is at a standstill now due to the sinkhole, and police are diverting road users away from the sea front so the rescue vehicles can get to the scene.

There are already 5 ambulances, 7 fire tenders and lots of police, and all these rescue crews are trying to get to the people down the sinkhole. Several local volunteer rescue teams have also joined in the rescue of the people trapped at the bottom of the 70ft deep sinkhole.

All around the sinkhole the crowd is watching these brave rescuer's as they descend down the deep hole, then someone comes over to them and says that Global Rescue are coming to help.

A woman in the crowd over hears this message and she spreads the news around the gathered crowd, and soon the whisper about Global Rescue coming has spread right along the sea front and the crowds are getting excited now.

The sea front has been cleared of any vehicles and barriers have been put all along the sea front, and as usual the crowds have gathered behind them. Two large TV screens have been set up and smaller ones are up all along the sea front so people can see what is going on at the sinkhole.

The news reporter has now heard about Global Rescue and she has her camera man and her crew get closer to the rollercoaster scene, because they know they will be stopping there. They know they will come down the sea front, and she wants her camera man to get them on the news. They know they won't be able to talk to them, but just knowing they are on their way is enough.

She stands opposite the Big One rollercoaster, where the people who are trapped are in view of the camera, and she starts another report.

"As you can see the trapped passengers are looking fine and not panicking and we are informed that volunteers are trying to get them food and drink but I'm not sure how they will do that." She looks directly at the camera now, a smile on her face. "And of course the big news now is that everyone here are awaiting the arrival of Global Rescue. We have been informed that they are approaching the sea front and should . . . ." She stops as she can hear loud sirens, and she looks down the sea front towards Blackpool tower and she sees a mass of red and orange flashing lights. She smiles at the camera, "It looks like Global Rescue are here, this is so exciting."

She gets the camera man to turn to the tower and film them coming down the sea front. The camera man swings round and gets them in the viewfinder as they come down the sea front in a mass of flashing lights. The crowds are clapping and cheering as they pass them.

The 2 road cruisers pull up just past all the fire tenders and ambulances to leave room for the other vehicles. The crane/ladder truck passes the crowds to loud cheering and clapping and for most people this is the first time they have seen them up close. Children are excited and clapping as loud as they can. The crane/ladder truck is the pride of the fleet and everyone loves this unusual and massive truck.

Next come the two 74ft long, 12ft wide super ambulances and everyone is in awe at their size too. The windows along the side are tinted black for privacy. People look at these amazing vehicles, then from above they hear the sound of high powered jet engines and they all look up. The camera man points his camera up.

He is amazed at what he sees in his viewfinder, and has to double check he's not dreaming. The crowds are all pointing up and even the rescue services look up too.

Above them the 2 airborne grapple jets have arrived and are hovering over the sinkhole, about 70ft up. These 162ft long jets have a set of 8 grapples which operate as one or, if needed, they can be used separately.

The crane/ladder truck pulls up almost opposite the news crew, and her camera man zooms in on the cab. Dave gets out of the cab to a tremendous cheer from the crowd, and on the coaster cars, even the passengers are cheering.

The chief of fire tender 4 comes over to him and shakes his hand. "Glad you got here so soon Dave."

"We knew this was very urgent so we got here as quick as we could." Dave smiles.

"So what's your plan, Dave?" I hope you have a plan Dave."

"I always have a plan chief." Dave looks up at the cars, and checks the structure over, then looks back at the chief. "Has there been any more movement in the structure chief?"

"No Dave, it seems to have settled now, but we didn't want to risk doing anything stupid."

"The plan I have come up with is we are going to use one of our grapple jets to get hold of the section of track the 6 cars are stuck on, then 4 of our top cutters will go up on the structure and cut the track section out, then we can lift it out and lower it on the beach."

"Why not use your ladder section on your truck to get them off?" the chief enquires.

"That would be a good idea under normal circumstances, but in this situation it's not. The ground could give way under the weight of our truck, and we could lose our truck and more importantly, those people up there."

The chief understands what he means. "I see Dave. I would never have thought of that."

"You would have done chief, but using the grapple jet means we can climb on the structure because it won't shake." He looks at his crews who are eager to get moving. "Well let's get on, these people look nervous." Dave gets out their portable comm device and looks up at the grapple jet. "This is Dave to Wesley, come in please."

"This is Wesley, go ahead Dave."

"I want you to lower the grapple and grab hold of the section of track the 6 coaster cars are on, but don't lift it, we need to cut it out first, OK?"

"No problem Dave. Lowering the grapples now." The crowd look up and watch as the jet hovers over the 6 coaster cars and then Wesley lowers the grapples slowly, and the passengers look up to see these huge grapples coming down. They all brace themselves, just in case.

On the ground the crowd are quiet as they watch this huge jet hovering over the stranded people, and they watch as the grapples get closer and closer. The news reporter sees this and gets the camera man to film this for the TV report.

Slowly the grapples pass the cars and the grapples have now been put on the same angle as the slope, and when it has passed the cars, the 8 hydraulic arms of the grapple close slowly and secure the track section.

The people in the cars sigh with relief as they now know they won't fall. Dave looks up and sees the track and cars are secure and gets back on the comm device. "Well done Wesley, perfect positioning. Now just hold the track securely till our cutter's have freed the track, then I'll give you the word and you can lift the track and cars over to the beach, OK."

"Ok Dave, I'll wait for you to tell me when." Wesley looks down at the track section and sees the people in the cars. He knows if he makes one mistake they will all fall into the sinkhole.

Dave has now gathered the rest of his teams at the crane/ ladder truck. "Ok, Ben, Jerry, Susan and Jenny you 4 climb up the structure and each of you cut one section of the track free, then signal me when it's done, Ok."

The four of them all say understood and off they go. Dave looks at the rest of his crew. "Ok could the rest of you help the other rescue services to get those trapped people out of the sinkhole?"

"Sure thing Dave" they all say together, and off they go. They make their way round the sinkhole and the crowd cheer as they pass them, and the other rescue service people are glad for the help.

The second airborne grapple jet has been hovering over the sinkhole all this time and everyone on the ground have wondered why. They all look up as the jet now moves directly over the centre of the sinkhole, and from beneath the jet they all see a huge open top container, and some wonder what this is for.

In the crowd a little girl sees the container and she asks one of the nearby Global Rescue crew members. "Excuse me sir" she asks in a soft voice.

"Yes, can I help you little miss?" Craig says to her as he stops beside her and her mother.

"What is that?" she says pointing up at the container. Craig looks up and smiles at her.

"That is our rescue basket miss. We are going to lower it down this hole, along with me and these rescue people, and we will use it to bring up those trapped people down there."

"Oh, right" she says smiling and with that Craig goes over to the rest of the crews. The basket is lowered and they all climb on board and the basket is then lowered down the sinkhole.

Dave stands next to the crane/ladder truck and watches his 4 crew climb up the structure to the trapped coaster passengers. The people see them climbing up and when all 4 of them are in position Jenny tells the passengers to turn away till they have cut the track rails free.

The 4 crew ignite their Hi Arc cutters and begin to cut through the tubular track. They cut through the track sections in a matter of minutes and on the ground the crew of fire tender 4 have been watching and they are impressed at the speed they cut through the track sections.

The 4 crew signal Dave that they have cut through the track and it's ready to be lifted and they stand on the track section with the passenger cars. Dave acknowledges them and gets onto Wesley. "Ok Wesley, the track is free, now lift slowly and when its free level out the section, then go to the beach, Ok?"

"Right Dave, lifting now." Everyone watches, holding their breaths, as the grapple jet raises up and the section of track with the 6 Cars on it breaks free from the rest of the structure. As the jet climb higher the crowds cheer and this can be seen right down the sea front on the Tv screens set up for people to watch.

The grapple jet flies over to the beach and in a cleared part of the busy beach, Wesley lowers the track and cars down slowly onto the sand, and when they are down safely, he opens the grapples and climbs higher and heads back to the sinkhole.

The people in the cars are a little stiff from sitting on an angle for so long and they have to get out slowly, but Global Rescue's ambulance crews come over and help them back to ambulance 1, for a check up.

# Chapter 4

———❦❖❦———

D ave and his crew now turn their attention to the
trapped people down the sinkhole, so they walk over to
the edge where he meets several volunteer rescuers.

The second grapple jet with the basket on it is hovering just
above them, and the basket has just come back to the surface
after dropping off the other rescue services at the bottom.

Dave opens the comm device and calls Raymond, the pilot
of grapple jet 1. "Ray can you lower the basket here so we can
get on board, then you can lower us all down the sinkhole.

Now the basket is large and can hold upto 20 adults, and
is very lightweight, and is held by 6 high grade steel cables. It
has a set of small doors at either end so access is easy.

Dave and the rest of his team stand back till the basket
is on the ground, they climb in, and Ray lifts them up and
lowers them down the sinkhole. As they are lowered slowly
down the sinkhole they can see the damage it has caused, with

bits of shops, rides and eating places all smashed and they line the wall of the hole.

They can see the ropes the volunteers have used to get down and Dave looks over the side of the basket and he can see many lights that the other rescue people are using. He turns the lights on that are on the bottom and sides of the basket and the whole area light up like daylight.

As they get closer to the bottom they can hear people calling out for loved ones or friends and most of them are in pain. When they reach the bottom they get out and start helping. As they move around the huge 300ft diameter of the hole, they notice several bodies covered over, and it's plain to see that some of them are children. Dave stands infront of the 8 bodies, 5 of which are children, and just looks at them. Jenny and Susan see Dave stood near the bodies, and as they get closer to him, they can see a tear in his eye.

"Are you alright Dave?" Jenny asks him as she puts her hand on his shoulder.

"I'm Ok Jenny, it's just seeing these bodies reminds me of the old days, in my mountain rescue days." He looks at her and smiles, then he spots one of the other rescue volunteers, and he goes over to him. "Hi there, so how many people do we have down here, at a rough guess?"

"I'd say about 200, maybe more. We haven't been able to dig in the rubble to see if anyone is still buried."

"Well I think the first thing we should do is get all the people who are able to move out of here, then we can have a bit of room so we can dig in and see if anyone is still buried, even if" and he looks at them all, "even if they are dead. I know we are going to find some more deceased people down here, buried in the rubble."

"I agree with you sir, we do need to get these people out of here in case this hole caves in on us." The man looks at Dave and Dave agrees on that. Both of them start getting people on the basket, and when it's full Ray lifts them to the surface, where they are met by all the ambulance crews.

An hour passes and all the movable people are out of the hole and now Dave, his crews and the other rescue people can begin digging others out.

They split into 7 teams of 4 and spread around the circumference of the sinkhole. Each team begins to dig to find anyone they can. It's not long before several people are found, a bit shaken but otherwise fine. They are taken to where the basket is waiting for them, and they all go to the surface.

Back on the surface the news reporter has been interviewing those that have come up, and most of them tell of seeing bodies covered up. The news is now going out live all down the sea front and on the TV stations and now everyone knows there are bodies down there.

Down in the sinkhole Dave and his team have just uncovered a family that where in one of the burger bars when it went down the sinkhole. They are covered in dirt and blood but no serious injuries. They are freed from the rubble and Jenny and Craig help them to the basket. All around the sinkhole the teams dig out lots of people and families.

Of course not every find is a happy one and Dave and his team come across the bodies of 4 children and 3 adults. Dave and his crew stand there, tears rolling down their faces at this awful sight, but they get them out, cover them over and put them with the others.

As time passes more bodies are found, and when they have finished the total count is 10 adults and 17 children. On the surface word has spread about the bodies and the crowds are sad and are waiting for news of who they are.

The basket is at the bottom of the sinkhole and now it's time to bring the bodies out. Dave tells the teams to put the adults on the basket first, and the other crews look at him puzzled.

Jenny goes over to him. "Why the adults first Dave?"

"As a sign of respect Jenny. We can't lift them all out at the same time because the basket won't hold all of them. The other rescuers can go up with the adults, and we will take the children up."

"Should we go and help them take them off at the surface?"

"No Jenny, these brave people can handle that, can't you?" Dave looks at the volunteers and they all agree they can. Jenny is still confused as to why Dave has left the children till last. Dave looks at her.

"The reason we ain't all going up to help Jenny is because I don't want to leave these poor children alone down here. I want to be here with them till we can get them to the surface, and I want the whole area up top clear."

"I'm with you now Dave. I understand" and she looks at Dave and he has tears in his eyes. Jenny hugs him and as they are hugging the adult bodies have been put on the basket.

Dave gets onto the chief, up on the surface. "Chief we are about to bring the adult bodies up so can you clear a space for them please?"

"Ok Dave, we'll get a space cleared for the bodies."

"Thanks chief." Dave looks at the bodies on the basket and he thanks all the volunteers for their help, and they shake his hand. "We'll see you all up there in a few minutes." They all look at Dave, then they look at the children's bodies, and the basket begins to rise upward.

A woman standing close to the chief has overheard the conversation with the chief and Dave. She taps him on his shoulder.

"Chief, did I hear them say they are bringing the bodies up now?"

"That's right. They are coming up now." The crowd around the hole go quiet, and look at the chief.

"Is it true that there are children among the dead chief?"

"I'm afraid that's true miss. I've been told that there are 10 adults and 17 children." He looks at the woman and then at the crowd who are now very quiet.

Around the sinkhole and all along the sea front the crowds now know the dead bodies are being brought up, and everyone is quiet. People along the sea front watch the Tv's as the first basket of dead bodies is raised. They all watch in silence and as the basket comes out of the sinkhole they all bow their heads in respect.

The basket is lowered gently to the ground and all the rescue services go and help take the bodies off, and they are taken to Global Rescue's super ambulance 2. The basket is lifted when it's empty and goes back down the hole.

Everyone now knows that this is for the children to be brought up. The news reporter tries to get close to the sinkhole and the chief spots her. He goes over to her, and he lets her through the barriers, and she thanks him. She wants the whole country to see these poor children being brought out of this sinkhole. They have already filmed the adult bodies being brought to the surface, and now they have to film the saddest part.

All around the sinkhole the crowd wait in total silence and down along the sea front even the owners of the noisy amusements have turned the music off as a sign of their respect.

Jenny and Dave are the only ones at the bottom of the sinkhole, looking at these poor children's bodies. Dave turns to Jenny. "Jenny I think we should both put the children on the basket one by one, with both of us carrying one child at a time."

"That sounds good to me Dave." She looks at him and smiles a bit. They both put the children onto the basket one at a time and when they are finished, Dave closes the small doors at the end of the basket, and Dave looks down at the children's bodies. He kneels down.

"Children, I'm sorry we couldn't save you, but you will be in our hearts, always." He looks at Jenny, a tear in his eyes, and Jenny has tears in hers too. "Sleep well little angels, the countries thoughts will be with you and your families."

Jenny starts to cry and Dave puts his arms around her and hugs her. "That was a nice thing to say Dave" she says as she hugs Dave too.

"It was said from the heart Jenny. I don't like to lose anyone on a rescue, but we were too late for these poor people." They break their hug and Dave gets Ray on the comm. "Ray, this is Dave we have the children on the basket now so you can lift us out, but do it slowly please Ray."

"Slow it is Dave, hold on please." The basket starts to rise up so Dave gets onto the chief.

"Chief, we're bringing the children up now, so stand by please."

"Ok Dave, the area is cleared and ready." The chief replies. On the surface the crowd has overheard the chief and Dave talking.

They can all see that the basket is on its way up, and they all hold hands in a chain around the sinkhole, and those on the sea front can see they have done this, so right down both sides of the main road the crowds have done the same.

The news reporter has stopped reporting and she has her camera man focus on the sinkhole, ready for the basket coming out. Around the sinkhole the crowd are told the basket is close to the top so they all bow their heads as the basket comes into view.

All the other rescue services do the same, and Ray lowers the basket gently to the ground. Everyone around the sinkhole has started crying or holding each other as the basket sits silent on the ground.

Along the sea front the crowds can see what is happening as the news reporter's camera man pans the camera round the crowd. The rescue volunteers and services all gather around the basket, ready to move the children's bodies to the Global Rescue's ambulance.

The camera man goes back to the basket and everyone goes quiet again. The crowd close to the sinkhole watch in total silence as all the rescue services take the children's bodies off the basket and carry them over to the ambulance, and all along the sea front they watch on the Tv screens.

When all the bodies are on the super ambulance, Dave gets the ambulance crew to one side. Dave goes over to Calvin, the driver of ambulance 2. "Calvin, take them to the hospital, but take it slow. The route has been cleared for you and you will have a police escort. When you have done that, meet us on the M6. Park in the nearest lay by and wait for us, Ok?"

"Right Dave, leave it to us." Dave pats him on his back and he and his crew climb onboard the super ambulance and close the doors. The tinted windows stop anyone seeing those inside, but everyone knows who is on the ambulance anyway.

The ambulance pulls away slowly and turns round to head for the sea front. The ambulance passes the crowd around the sinkhole again, and they all have their heads bowed in respect.

Right down the sea front the people have been told the ambulance with the bodies on is due to pass them shortly. The word has got round and now the entire route to the hospital has been lined with people, all holding hands as a sign of respect.

People along the sea front all want to see the ambulance pass, so they find anything to stand or sit on that will give them a view. As the ambulance passes them they all bow their heads, and even children do the same, and no one says a word. The ambulance travels down the sea front in total silence, other than the sea gulls squawking away, escorted by 2 police cars.

The ambulance arrives at the hospital, and as the ambulance stops outside the hospital, the doctors and nurses come out to help take the bodies off. They all know who they are because they have been watching the Tv reports.

Calvin and the crew all thank the doctors and nurses for their help then get back on their ambulance. Calvin looks at his crew before he sits down. "Thank you everyone, a good job and well done." He gets in the driver's seat and they leave the hospital grounds.

Outside the gates the crowds are still there and as a sign of respect for this brave crew, they clap and cheer them as they head for the M6.

Back at the sinkhole the crowds are chatting again and all the rescue and volunteers are stood with Dave and his crews. They thank Global Rescue for their help and everyone shakes hands and says farewell.

"Thanks for all your help Dave, it was much appreciated." The chief shakes Dave's hand.

"No problem chief, and if you ever need us, just call." Dave smiles at him.

As they are doing this, the people from the rollercoaster cars come over to Dave and his crew. The men, women and children all thank the Global Rescue crews for getting them off the ride safely, and they shake their hands too.

Dave is very proud of his crews and he thanks them too, then they get back on their vehicles. The crowd are now waiting for them to pass by them, and the children all want to see them too, so adults lift them onto their shoulders to get a good view.

Global Rescue drive down the sea front to clapping and cheering and they all wave back to the crowds as they pass, then when they are out of the boundary, the vehicles head for the M6 and home. As they come to the slip road they see their ambulance, so Dave blows the horn and they join at the back of the convoy and Global Rescue head for home and a well earned rest and a cuppa.

The End

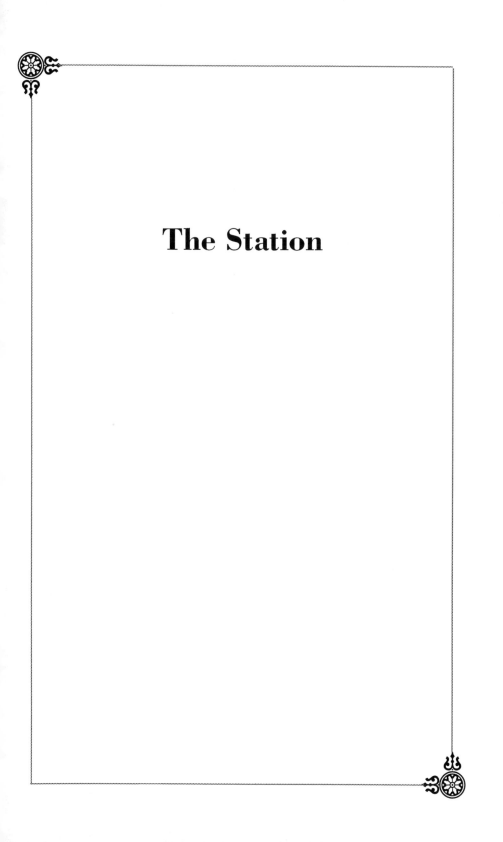

# The Station

# Chapter 1

It's a very stormy night and the gang are all on their way home from a day out at Blackpool. Martin, Sarah, Donna and Vicky travel in two cars, Martin's and Sarah's, as they head home to Hull. These friends are all roughly the same age, all in their thirties.

They have another friend called John, but he was not with them on this day out because he had to go to a meeting at work, up in Carlisle. He wanted to go to Blackpool with his friends but work called him in at the last minute.

The rain is pouring down as Martin and Sarah drive back to Hull, and the storm has now produced a thunderstorm, and as the lightning flashes and the thunder rumbles across the night sky, Martin and Sarah are finding it hard to drive.

The rain gets harder and harder and the roads start to flood, making the driving very hard. All their cars are fitted with a CB radio system so they can keep in contact. Vicky in

Martins car, and Donna is with Sarah and she cringes every time the lightning flashes, and Vicky doesn't like thunder at all. Vicky looks at martin as he concentrates on the road.

"I wish John was here" she says a little scared now, "I would feel a lot better if I was with him in his car." Martin hears this and glances at her.

"Oh thanks, I'm not that bad a driver am I?"

"No, course you aren't Martin" she says to reassure him, "I miss John that's all." Vicky and John are together in the sense of a relationship and they love each other and the others know this.

Martin drives on and as he does he picks up the CB radio mic and gets on to Sarah, who is behind him.

"Sarah I think we should find somewhere to stop till this storm passes."

"We just checked the map and there is a station just ahead, should we stop there?" Sarah looks at Donna as she waits for Martin to reply. Martin and Sarah are also in a relationship and have been for over a year or so.

The rain begins to get heavier and so Martin decides they will pull into the station. "I think we had better pull into this station, I can't see the road because of all this rain. Follow me Sarah."

"OK" comes over the CB from Sarah, and Martin spots the station as a huge flash of lightning lights it up. Martin drives into the small station and the road drops slowly into a small car park.

In his headlights he can see the station and it looks derelict and old. The rain is so heavy now that it runs down the slope of the car park and off the end of the old platform.

There is a huge flash of lightning and a loud clap of thunder, and Sarah and Donna look around the station as it is briefly lit up. They all get out of the two cars and shelter under part of the old stations overhead canopy.

It is very dark when there is no lightning, then all of a sudden there is a big flash of lightning and they all jump. They all see that there is a tunnel at the side of the station and it has been boarded up. The rain pours so they look round for a way in. Vicky comes across a door and she tries it, and the door opens, squeaking as it does.

"That sounds creepy" Donna says as she walks into the old stations waiting room. She brushes several cob webs out of her face as she walks into the open area of the room. "It smells damp in here."

"What do you expect Donna?" Sarah says as she walks past her, "It's raining heavily out there and this old place won't be water tight anymore."

"I recon this place has been in this state for a very long time you lot" Martin says as he looks round. The main window onto the platform is still intact and let's light in, but the gang start looking to see if they can find any candles.

Donna opens a drawer and peers in, and as she does a huge spider crawls out and onto the counter and she screams out. The others look round quickly.

"Whats wrong Donna?" Sarah shouts to her. Donna is still getting her breath back and she sees it is only a spider.

"Nothing" she says calm now, "it was only a spider." Martin looks across at her laughing.

"I didn't know you were afraid of spiders Donna" he says still laughing, "You told me they never bother you."

"Shut up Martin" she replies, "it took me by surprise."

Over in the corner of the room, Vicky opens another drawer and steps back just in case another spider crawls out, because she hates spiders. She opens the drawer fully and sees there are several candles in it. "I've found some candles" she tells the rest.

"Great" Martin says as he goes over to her and the two of them gather the candles up and go over to the main waiting room desk. All of them take a candle or two each and light them then use the wax to stick them in various places around the room so it lights up the room.

The candles bathe the room in a pale yellow glow and as the flames flicker from the wind outside, they all look at the strange shadows they cast. The gang now look round the rest of this building and come across some chairs and a table, so they move them into the waiting room.

There is a coal fire on the back wall of the room, and this looks as if it hasn't been used for years, but to their surprise there are still some logs in the corner, so they put three on the fire.

"What we need now is some paper to get it started." Martin says and they all look round for some. Vicky goes through another door they never tried and comes into a small kitchen, and in the centre is a wood burning stove. Next to the stove are some more logs and a stack of papers.

"Hey you lot, I've found some paper and a wood burning stove too." Donna, Martin and Sarah look at each other then go to Vicky. They look round the small kitchen as a flash of lightning lights it up through the skylight in the roof.

"Everyone, get a handful of papers and follow me" Martin says as he picks some of the papers up. The others do the same and they all go into the main room and over to the fire. The girls all screw the papers up into tight bundles and Martin get a lighter out. The girls put the paper around the logs and Martin lights them all.

It takes a couple of minutes for them to catch, but soon the fire is ablaze and the gang sit round it to get warm. Vicky stands up quickly and they all look at her.

"What is it Vicky?" Sarah asks her.

"I just had a thought" she says looking down at her friends. "How is John going to know where we are, he will think we have gone home." She looks at them all and they look at each other.

"We could bring one of the CB radio's in here then if he finds we ain't at home he will contact us. Martin, can you get yours out your car please?"

"Sure" he says and gets up.

"We might aswell get the rest of the picnic stuff too" Sarah says.

"I'll give you a hand." The two of them leave the two other girls in the station room, sat near the fire.

Outside there is no let-up in the storm as Martin and Sarah dash to the car. Martin un-hooks the CB radio while Sarah gets the picnic stuff.

They head back to the waiting room when a big flash of lightning lights up the entire station and Martin looks at the tunnel then he looks over the side of the platform as another flash of lightning lights everything up. He sees there are no rails at the side of the platform. A huge and very loud clap of thunder shakes the station and Sarah runs back in and Martin follows her.

"I think it's getting worse out there you lot, I recon we will be here all night. The rain is running off the platform like a waterfall." He looks at the girls, all sat round the fire with the picnic hamper. "Oh just to let you know I saw there were no rails at the side of the platform and there is a small door into the tunnel."

The girls mutter something and carry on pouring the drinks and setting out the sandwiches on the table. Martin sets the CB up on the waiting room counter and turns it on, but doesn't notice he has turned the volume down. No one is on the CB at the moment because they have their own channel that they all agreed on so they can keep in contact, and which they all know off by heart.

Sarah looks round the room and the candles cast strange and scary shadows. "This place gives me the creeps" she says and the girls look at her.

"It will be alright in here, at least we are warm and dry, and I don't think we will get any visitors, not in this weather. Martin has got a torch from the car and so he goes off on a little adventure while the girls talk.

He goes over to the front window and looks out. Small lightning flashes show the station off and on the far side of the station there is an embankment covered in grass and trees. He looks round every time it lightens and takes note of anything he can see.

# Chapter 2

Miles away, up near Carlisle John has just set off in his Ford Cortina Mk 2 car, heading home. The storm is still going strong, even up here and the weather reports on the radio say that this storm is the worst one in recent records, and is set to last at least another twelve hours or so.

John pulls onto the M6 motorway and heads for Blackpool and he hopes he will meet up with his friends there, but he doesn't know they left when the storm started. The storm has now gathered a strong wind, and on the open motorway the driving conditions are awful, and John is finding it hard to keep on the road.

He knows Vicky will be scared and so he wants to get to her so he knows she is safe. John picks up the CB mic and tunes it to channel 77.

"This is John to the gang can you hear me, over?" He listens but all he hears is static. He tries again and waits.

Back at the station one of the girls hears a faint voice and looks round. Vicky and Sarah look at Donna as she is still looking round.

"Can you hear that?" she asks them.

"Hear what, Donna?" asks Sarah.

"It sounded like someone talking very faintly." Donna looks round the room again and she hears it again. "There, did you hear it that time?" She looks all over the room, and Vicky is now looking as she heard it too.

"It's your imagination Donna. There won't be anyone out in this weather."

Vicky shushes her and Sarah looks at her amazed. "No, Donna's right, I can hear it too." Over in the corner they hear the faint sound again and Vicky knows that voice. "It's John" she says as she runs over to the CB. "It's John on the CB." She looks at the CB and notices it has been turned down.

"This is John to the gang, I'm on my way to meet you in Blackpool, so let me know where you are."

"Hi John, this is Vicky." Martin comes back in the room and sees Vicky talking on the CB, and he goes over to Donna and Sarah.

"Whats going on?" he asks them.

"It's John on the CB. He is on his way to meet us." Sarah looks at Martin who is a bit confused.

"Coming to meet us? but he doesn't know where we are. In fact even I don't know where we are. Sarah can you use the map and find out please?"

"Sure" she says smiling at him, "I have a rough idea as to where we are." She and Donna get the map out and put it on the table and check their route. Vicky is still talking to John.

"So where are you now John?"

"Not far from Blackpool, on the M6, but the storm is making driving a nightmare. I can't see a bloody thing in this rain, and I only get a glance of the road when it lightens."

"Oh be careful won't you, darling." She now feels a bit less scared now she knows John is on his way.

"Course I will sweetheart, don't worry. Is Martin there?"

"Yeah he's right here, I'll put him on." Vicky hands the mic to Martin.

"So mate how's it going?"

"Not good, this bloody rain and wind is terrible here on the motorway. Are you all still in Blackpool?"

"No mate we left when the storm started but we had to stop on the way, and we are in a small derelict station."

"Where?" John wants to get to them before he is blown off the road or worst still, if the roads are closed.

"Hang on, I'll find out." He turns the mic off and in his car John drives cautiously in the super storm. Martin goes over to Sarah and Donna. "Do you know where we are yet?"

"Yeah, we're here at a place called Holme Chapel, on the A646." Martin goes back to the CB and picks the mic up.

"John, are you still there?"

"Yep still here. Just had a little excitement here on the motorway, a tree has blown down across one of the lanes and a lorry had hit it. I don't think anyone was hurt, but this storm is getting worse."

"We are at a place called Holme Chapel on the A646, in the small station just over the humpbacked bridge."

"Right, you all stay there and I'll be there as soon as I can. Don't come looking for me." He wants to make sure they don't do something foolish, like come out to find him, because in this storm they could pass each other in the dense rain. The CB goes quiet and Martin goes over to the girls.

Sarah looks at him. "Is John on his way here?"

"Yeah, he said we should stay put and not go out looking for him, and he'll be here as soon as he can."

Donna looks at them all. "I bet the weather isn't much better where John is. It seems to be getting worse too."

Martin looks at Vicky and can see she is looking nervous at what Donna has just said. "The storm is the same all down this side of the country according to the weather reports." He looks at Donna and Sarah as they are a little confused as to where he got this information, but as they look at him he nods over to Vicky over near the fire, and they now know what he means.

"John's a good driver, he'll be fine. He's driven in worse than this when he was a heavy haulage driver." Sarah says as she goes over to her worried friend, she put her arm round Vicky and Vicky looks at her reassuring smiling face. "John will be fine Vicky, don't you worry about that."

"I know he'll be alright but I still worry about him." She looks at Sarah and Sarah knows something else is on her mind. Donna sees them near the fire and goes over to them.

"Anything wrong here?" she asks politely.

Vicky looks at them both and smiles. "John has asked me to marry him" she says softly and the two of them shout out in excitement, and Martin hears them and comes over.

"What did you say Vicky?" he asks, knowing exactly what she said, but he wants to be sure.

"I said John has asked me to marry him." She looks at the three of them and they all have a huge smile on their faces.

"That's great news Vicky, great news indeed" Sarah says to her as she gives her a hug. Donna and Martin also give her a hug and she feels a lot better now. The four of them sit down at the table and finish off their sandwiches and coffee as the pale glow from the burning fire lights the room up with a romantic looking setting.

They talk about their day in Blackpool as the thunder, lightning and rain carry on outside. The gang can hear the heavy rain on the roof of the station, and they feel better knowing they are warm and dry, but Vicky thinks about John, all alone on the motorway in this storm.

"So Donna what was your best part of the day then?" Martin asks her.

"That has to be when we went on the big rollercoaster. It was a great ride on that, and made better with you all there. Mind you it was scary in places, but it was still good." Donna has a small smile on her face.

"So what about you Sarah, what did you enjoy about today?"

"Er well it was the amusements. I like them and I know it's a waste of money, but they're fun." Martin looks at Vicky and she is just stirring out the main window at the storm.

He decides to not ask her yet, and he goes into the kitchen. He looks round and spots some old newspapers they never used and he picks them up. He goes back into the waiting room and he sits down to read them.

The girls are all sat round the fire, and the main conversation is about John and Vicky. "Vicky when did he ask you to marry him?" Donna enquires.

"It was about two weeks ago, when we went to Bridlington for the day. We was walking along the beach and eating an ice cream, if I remember correctly, and it was nice and sunny, and when we stopped near the water's edge he just came out with it."

"I bet it took you by surprise eh?" Sarah asks her. "I think none of us expected John to do that. Oh we know he loves you dearly, and he would do anything to make you happy, but this is a big surprise to all of us."

"I stood there in a state of shock for a few seconds and he asked me again and I smiled at him and said yes." They all look at Vicky, even Martin and they stand up and hug her again.

"You will make a great couple you two, and it will be the best wedding ever, we'll see to that won't we Donna?" Sarah says to her and she agrees.

# Chapter 3

On the M6, John is battling the storm as he heads towards his friends. He reaches the junction turn off onto the M62 and he takes the exit. The rain is very heavy here and his car has trouble finding grip on the flooded surface, but he manages to find some grip and he joins the A677 towards Blackburn. He knows the gang are waiting for him so he tries to speed up, but the weather limits this as the rain batters his car and the wind plays it part too.

In the station's waiting room the gang are keeping warm as the temperature starts to fall and Martin looks at the gauge and sees it has already dropped a couple of degrees.

Donna gets up and checks a couple of the other rooms out, looking for the toilet, but she can't find it. "Wonder where the toilet is in this station?" she says to the rest of them. Martin looks up from the newspapers he's reading at Donna.

"I think they are outside and along the platform." He looks at Donna as she heads for the door. "You had best take this torch so you can see your way."

Donna takes the torch and goes outside. She stays under the canopy, trying to keep out of the rain, but the wind blows it along the platform and she starts getting wet. She shines the torch on every door she sees and she finds the ladies toilet, and she goes in.

The toilet smells dank and the place isn't exactly the best place but she needs the loo. The lightning is now more intense than ever and the toilet is lit up by flash after flash and she looks round the old toilet, and there is a bit of damage but on the whole it's not too bad. When she has finished she leaves the toilet and heads back to the waiting room.

She is only a few yards away from the waiting room when a long flash of lightning lights up the entire platform, tunnel and embankment and she spots a dark figure on the edge of the platform.

"Hello, who is that?" there is no reply from the figure, and the station goes back into darkness. Another flash of lightning lights the station up, and Donna sees the figure has gone. She goes into the waiting room and sees all her friends there.

Sarah sees the expression on her face. "What's up Donna?" she asks curious.

"Have any of you just been out on the platform?" she looks at them, hoping one had.

"No one has left the room except you." Martin says as he looks at her worried face. "Why? Did you see someone out there?"

"I think so. There was a black figure stood on the edge of the platform, and I thought it was one of you waiting for me to return."

"Well Donna none of us has been out there, not in this weather." Martin gets up and goes over to her and puts his arm around her and she is shaking. "Come and sit down and have some hot coffee." He looks at her and she sits down with the other girls. "Perhaps there was someone out there Donna, but no one came in here" and he pauses, "but if there was someone out there they must be mad to be out in this."

Sarah turns to Martin, "Maybe it was someone just came down here to go to toilet, but couldn't be bothered to go to the toilet building or was caught short."

"That would explain a lot eh?" Martin sits down and carries on reading. Vicky gets up and walks over to the window and there is another flash of lightning and she sees the black figure on the edge of the platform.

"Good god" she screams out, and points out the window. The rest of them look at her then out the window.

"What? What did you see Vicky?" Martin asks her.

"The black figure is out there. Someone is out there watching us."

"I can't believe anyone would want to be out in this just to watch us having some sandwiches and coffee." They all look out the window as another flash lights the platform up, and the figure has gone.

"There is no one there now" says Sarah and they all turn away from the window, all except Martin. There is another flash of lightning and he sees the black figure.

"She's right, look, there it is." They all turn quickly and see the black figure at the edge of the platform. The station goes into darkness until the next flash of lightning, and when it comes they all see the figure has gone.

"If someone is playing silly tricks here then I'm going to go out there and tell them off because they are upsetting the girls." He opens the door and goes outside.

Over near the fire, Sarah and Vicky are sat keeping warm, and chatting to each other. "So Vicky, John has asked you to marry him eh? I'll tell you that is the best news I've heard for a long time."

"I was a bit scared at the time but when I sat and thought about it, you know the first time he asked me that is, then when he asked me again I knew I wanted to marry him." She looks at Sarah and she has a small tear in her eyes. "Are you alright Sarah?" Vicky asks just in case she is upset or something.

"I'm fine, I'm fine" she says sniffing a bit and brushing a tear away from her eye. She looks at Vicky with a reassuring look and they both turn to the fire and warm their hands.

Martin is stood on the rain soaked platform, and Donna is stood behind the closed door watching. There is a flash of lightning and there on the edge of the platform is the dark figure, and Martin can see the figure is hooded and slightly bent over looking at where the rails would have been.

"Hey you" he shouts to the figure, "you there, you're frightening the girls in the waiting room" and he waits for an answer. The lightning flash ends and the station is in darkness again but almost instantly there is another flash and Martin sees the figure has gone.

He is soaked now so heads back to the door and as he does he hears a very faint whistle, far off in the distance. Donna waits for him to come in then notices he hasn't so she looks out the window and sees he is stood on the platform looking to the side of the building. She is puzzled so she goes outside.

Martin sees her come out and turns to her. "What are you doing out here Donna? It's chucking it down. Go back inside."

She turns back to the door then she hears the whistle off in the distance. She looks at Martin and he looks at her. "You heard that too eh?"

"I sure did. What do you think it is?" she stands with him in the rain, both of them at the edge of the platform.

"Not sure" he pauses to see if it sounds again and sure enough the whistle sounds, but now it's getting closer. "It sounds like the whistle of an old steam train" and he looks over the platform, and so does Donna, and they can see there are no rails alongside the platform.

"I wonder if there is one close by and we can hear it here?"

"As far as I know there are no main line railways close by. I was reading in those old newspapers that most of the railway lines round this area where closed a long time ago, due to cut backs it says."

The whistle sounds again and this time it is a longer blast and they both know it's getting closer. "This is weird" Donna says and she heads back to the waiting room. She goes in and Martin turns to go in an in the next flash of lightning he sees the dark figure again, and it seems to be looking striaght at him. He looks at the creepy vision, and slowly moves to the door, watching the figures hooded face as he does. He sees that the head never moves, and he can see it is looking down the track towards the sound of the whistle.

Martin walks slowly over to the figure and as he nears it, the head moves to face him. The lightning is now continuous and Martin has a good look at this strange figure.

"Look mate if you're trying to frighten us all you're doing a damn good job. Why don't you come in the station and get warm and dry." The figured person doesn't reply, then the wind blows the hood off the figures head and Martin looks at it.

The face is very old and the skin is so tight the face looks more like bone than flesh. Martin looks very closely at the figure and he makes out that it is a woman, but that's not what is worrying him at the moment, because he can see all the facial features of a person, but the head is see through.

Donna comes back to the window when she notices that Martin hasn't come back in yet. She looks through the stained and dirty window and sees Martin close to the dark figure. The station goes back into darkness and a very loud clap of thunder cracks overhead and Martin runs in and Donna notices the figure has gone.

Martin opens the door, runs in, and slams it shut behind him, and this disturbs Sarah's concentration. "What's up with you? You look as if you have just seen a ghost" and she laughs but she notices he isn't laughing. Sarah and Vicky get up and go over to him and Donna near the window. "What's wrong?"

"That dark figure out there" he pauses to get his breath back, "well it's no ordinary person. I got a good look at it and that my friend's is what we call a ghost."

"A ghost?" asks Vicky. "Are you sure Martin? Let's face it here, it's a pretty creepy night out there with all the thunder, lightning and heavy rain, but saying to us that it's a ghost, come on we all like a prank now and again, but this is too much."

"Oh believe me I aren't making this up, that" and he points out the window, "is a ghost."

"I believe him" Donna says as they all stand near the window.

"Well that would explain how it can appear and disappear quickly." They all walk over to the table and Martin pours himself a coffee and sits down. The rest of them sit and look at Martin, who is in a state of shock, but aware of everything too.

"That's not all either" he says swallowing a mouth full of coffee, "there is the whistle." Sarah and Vicky look at him stunned.

"Whistle?" Sarah asks curious. "What whistle?"

"Donna and I heard the whistle of a steam train off in the distance, but it started to get closer."

"It's true" Donna tells them both, "we did hear a train whistle and it was heading this way." Sarah and Vicky look at them both and think they are playing a prank, when the train whistle sounds again, and this time it sounds really close by.

"I heard that" Sarah says nervously, "and it sounds really close." While they are all talking Donna has gone to the window, and to her shock she sees the dark figure on the platform, but there is no lightning, and the figure is now surrounded by an eerie glow and she calls them all over.

They rush to the window and they all see the figure at the edge of the platform, looking down the line. They all go outside cautiously and keep looking at the figure, then there is a bright light coming from the right of the station, and they hear the train whistle.

The platform begins to shake and they grab hold of anything that is solid enough to take their weight. The waiting room shakes and they all look down the track and there they see a huge steam train heading for them.

"This is impossible" Martin shouts out over the sound of the train, "there are no bloody tracks here." They all back away from the platform edge and stand with their backs to the waiting rooms big window.

The dark figure jumps off the platform as the steam train passes the station, and the gang all get a good look at it, and they can see right through the train as it passes them. There are a row of bright lights where the windows would be and the gang stand in amazement as the train rumbles past them.

"What the hell is going on here?" Donna asks them.

"Got me, I have no idea what the hell is going on." Sarah says to them all.

Vicky looks at Martin. "Just to confirm one thing, that was a ghost train we have just seen, wasn't it?"

"It certainly looked like one to me." Martin says to Vicky." I'll tell you one thing though I've never seen anything like that in my life."

Sarah walks to them as they stand in the rain. "One thing still puzzles me though" she says, and they all look at her in anticipation. "Who was the figure in black?"

The train goes through the boarded up part without damaging anything too, and the gang are stunned. When the train has passed the station goes dark again. Martin checks over the platform where the figure jumped but sees nothing at all.

The gang head back into the waiting room when all of a sudden there is a loud noise from the tunnel, and they all turn to look.

"What on earth was that?" Sarah says out loud. Then there is another loud noise and they all look at each other. "Good god that doesn't sound good."

Martin looks at the girls a little worried. "It sounds like the train has crashed, but that second noise baffles me." They stand in the pouring rain pondering what Martin said, then from in the waiting room they hear a voice.

"Do you hear that?" Donna asks them. "It's coming from the waiting room." Donna listens to hear it again but Vicky runs past her and the others are wondering whats up. They all go back into the waiting room and see Vicky is on the CB. She looks at them all as they come back in.

"It's John" she says excited.

"Hi all I'm not far away now. I'm still trying to find this Holme Chapel place, but in this rain and lightning nothing is easy to see."

Vicky uses the CB mic. "You be careful darling, just get here as soon as you can." He senses slight fear in her voice.

"Are you alright sweet heart, you sound a little scared."

"I'm fine John, don't worry. The weather is scary though, and the rain is now starting to flood down the end of the platform."

"Well dear I'll be there shortly so don't you worry yourself. Sit down, have a coffee and something to eat, and I'll be there before you know it."

"OK I'll do that dear. See you soon." The CB goes quiet and the gang sit down at the table and have a drink. They all chat about what they have just seen and they are all puzzled as to what is going on.

"I wonder why that train passed here today? Is it just because the weather is bad, or are we all drunk and imagined it?"

"I know I'm not drunk, and I did imagine what I saw and heard. Something happened here at this station, I'm sure of it."

"Hey that's probably why the railway lines have been taken up and why there are no more trains to this station anymore." Martin looks round the room and spots the pile of newspapers he was reading and goes to get them. The girls stay close to the fire to stay warm, and Martin returns with the papers.

"There might be something in these papers that might explain what happened here. All of them take a couple of papers each and read through them."

Everyone has several papers by their side and they read through them carefully. Outside the rain is coming down hard and it bounces off the roof of the waiting room, and the thunder has now grown in strength, and each loud clap of thunder shakes the waiting room, but the gang are getting used to that.

They read the papers then Sarah comes across the article they are looking for. "Here, I think this is it." They all get up and go over to her and she lays the paper open on the table.

Martin gets his torch and holds it up high so it lights the paper up for them all to read. The paper is just readable and Martin looks at the headline. "It says, train wreck at Holme chapel station, and its dated 1957." He looks at the girls and they look as puzzled as he does. "It goes on to say there was a train crash in the tunnel, and the train was so badly damaged, and the carriages where thrown off the rails and got so tightly jammed in the tunnel they were unable to get them out and clear the wreckage because the wreckage is so far into the tunnel."

Martin takes a sip of coffee and carries on. "It goes on to say that the crash was a mystery till about a month later when they found the dismembered body of an old lady, dressed in black, and they think she fell onto the tracks at the station and her body was dragged along by the train." Martin looks at the girls and they look puzzled again, then Sarah realises something.

"Hey that old lady must be the dark figure we have been seeing on the platform.

"Do you think she was the cause of the accident?" Vicky asks.

"We can't be certain of that now, can we?" Martin says reading the article again.

"We saw her fall onto the tracks though, didn't we?" Vicky says still reading the paper.

"Ah but she never fell onto the tracks, she jumped into the path of the train." Sarah replies.

"That's true" Martin says finishing the article again. "Mind you a person jumping into the path of a train wouldn't derail it" he looks at them, "No there must have been something else, but what?"

The girls look at him and shrug their shoulders as they have no idea either.

"Whatever caused that crash is in that tunnel. It looks like they never found out what really caused it, so they sealed the tunnel up, and it's been like that since 1957." Martin looks through the paper to see if there is any more about it, but there isn't.

"Yeah but the rescue services of the time should have found the real cause, but obviously they didn't and they never had the time to go over the wreckage fully." Vicky looks at them and smiles a bit.

They check through all the papers and Vicky comes across another article, written two months later.

"Here we are, this one was written two months after the one we just read." She looks at them all.

"What does it say?" Sarah asks Vicky.

"Well . . . it says the rescue services couldn't get right into the tunnel because they were limited to what they could do at the time, so they just left all the passengers and the train in the tunnel. They could hear no sounds and just thought that everyone had died in the crash. The tunnel was boarded up and the rails removed and the railway line was diverted round Holme chapel."

"Well that says it all eh?" Martin says as he walks away from the table.

"Fancy leaving all those people in there, surely they could have got the bodies out by now." Sarah looks at the paper and realises that it has been 22 years since the crash and no one has even bothered to reclaim the bodies.

"Perhaps it was too dangerous, and with the train so well jammed in the tunnel, they just couldn't get to them." Donna says as she finishes reading the page. They all agree to that being the reason and sit and have a drink.

# Chapter 4

The storm continues and John has just gone past Burnley and is now on the A646. The lightning and the rain continue to be a problem, but he soon sees the boundary marker for Holme Chapel and he looks out for the humpbacked bridge.

There is a flash of lightning and he sees the bridge just ahead and in the next flash he spots the old station. John slows his car as he nears the bridge and once over he makes a sharp left into the car park. He pulls into the car park and the headlights from his car light up the waiting room, and the gang look out to see what it is.

Sarah runs to the window. "It's John" she shouts out and Vicky leaps to her feet, and the others get up too. They all go to the window, and through the dirty window they see John getting out his car. He runs from his car to the door and comes in.

Vicky is there to greet him and she throws her arms around him and gives him a big kiss. He looks at her. "Now that's what I call a welcome" and he and all the gang laugh, but Vicky still keeps her arms round him. He puts his arms around her and holds her close, and she nestles her head on his shoulder and she feels so safe now. "God this weather is awful and the journey here was scary, fallen trees and power lines down, but I got here." He laughs but the gang stay quiet. "Hmm, tough crowd" he says trying to lighten the mood. "So anything good happened to you lot while you've been here?"

They all look at each other and John is puzzled, then they all look at John. "Well some strange events have unfolded in the past couple of hours here and we have been checking the papers for information." Martin looks at John, his long-time friend, and sort of smiles.

"What sort of strange events?" he asks him and Martin is stuck for the right words then Donna notices the dark figure is back on the platform.

"Hey look" she says pointing to the window, "the dark figure of that old lady is back again." Everyone looks out the window and John sees it too, and he goes over to the door to go and find out, but the gang stop him.

"Why did you stop me she might need help?" he says looking at them.

"That old lady is a ghost" Donna says as they look at John.

"A ghost?" he says curiously. "Really?" he says as they look at him. "Come on you lot, stop pulling my leg here."

"I know it sounds funny, but trust us, we know what we are saying is true." Just then they all hear the whistle of the train again, and it sends a chill down their spines because they know what is about to happen. "This has all happened before, about an hour ago."

"Here comes the train again" Sarah says to him. "This is so strange."

"Why is that Sarah?" John asks curiously.

"Well we have seen the train come past before." Sarah looks very frightened now, and Martin holds her hand to comfort her.

"What" he says astonished. "When was that?"

"It was about half an hour ago dear" Vicky says looking at him, a small smile on her face.

John looks at them and from their facial expressions he knows they are telling the truth. "So you think it's going to come past again?"

"Wait and see, John, wait and see." They all go outside and John looks at the dark cloaked figure and then he feels the platform start to shake, then the station starts shaking just like last time.

The train whistle gets louder as it closes in on the station and the platform shakes even more than last time. They all look down the track and see a bright light approaching and they stand back and hold onto each other's hands. The train screams past the station and in the midst of it all, John sees the figure jump off the platform into the path of the train. Vicky squeezes his hand as the train passes and he knows she is scared.

"See, we told you strange things have been going on here."

"So I can see. That train was certainly transparent, and not a normal train. Did any of you notice that the train made no sound as it went past us, and there wasn't even any wind from it?" He looks at them and they all look at him puzzled. "Have we any clues on why this train is doing this?"

"We have some newspaper articles on the train crash, and it all happened in 1957." Donna looks at John and she smiles.

"Where are these papers? I'd like to have a read of them." John and the gang walk back into the waiting room.

"The papers are on the table" Martin says, "do you want a coffee?"

"That would be the ticket mate" and John starts to read the articles concerning the train crash. They hear the train crashing inside the tunnel, and John looks at them. "Did it do that the last time too?" he asks all of them, and they shake their heads in agreement.

John sits at the table while Martin makes them all a coffee and the girls sit around the table. John reads the papers and as he does he starts to put all the events together, and when he's finished he sits back in the old creaky chair and takes a sip of his coffee.

"It says in the last report that this train has been heard several times on this particular night over the years, and witnesses say they have heard cries and screams from the tunnel after the crashing sound was heard."

"So what does that mean John?" Donna asks as she sips her coffee.

"Well to me it means only one thing." He looks at everyone.

"And that is what exactly?" Martin enquires.

"Their souls are not at rest" he says as he closes the papers. The girls all look at him and they are puzzled at his statement. Martin sits down opposite him and he looks over to John and he is curious.

"So if that's true, what can we do?" John looks at him, then at the girls and smiles.

"We have to go into the tunnel, find all the remains of those poor people and bury them in a single grave then they can finally rest in peace."

"Do you think that's why this keeps happening?" Sarah asks him.

"I certainly do." He looks at them all sat there and outside the rain still pours, and now they can hear strange noises from the tunnel. They never heard them before and they look at John for answers.

"How do you come to that conclusion then?" Martin asks him.

"Did you fully read these papers reports? It says that this train crash has been going on since 1957, and no one knew why so they boarded up the tunnel, removed the lines and closed the station all because of this crash. It went on to say that many families who lived close to this station moved away because of these strange events, and it ends with the report that because they never managed to recover the bodies of the crash victims, people around the area had the tunnel boarded up and they just left them in there. There has been no memorial service for these people, and I believe that is why this happens every year."

The gang look at him, astonished, and after it has sunk in they also realise this is why this keeps happening now. Vicky looks at John.

"So you're saying that these people need to be gathered and buried in a grave, and this will end the train crash for them?"

"Spot on dear." He looks at them all. While they have been talking the rain has begun to ease and there is no more thunder and lightning. John gets up and goes to the window and outside he can see that dawn is about to break, and there is a faint glow of the sun on the tops of the trees on the opposite embankment.

John looks at the tunnel and he sees a service door close to the end of the platform, and he turns to his friends. "I have an idea" he says and they all look at him.

"What?" asks Donna and Martin at the same time.

"Why don't we see if we can end this torment for the crash victims." They look at him, their mouths open.

"How do we do that?" Martin says, already having an idea what he's going to say next.

"Well we go into the tunnel and find all the bones of every victim and we dig a grave and bury them all together. That way their spirits can rest in peace."

They look at him, thinking he's joking with them, but they see he has a serious face. "You're kidding of course" Donna asks him, hoping she's right this once.

"No" he says abruptly. "I know it sound odd and creepy, but we witnessed an event here last night that has been going on for the past twenty two years, and I think it's time for it to end for these poor people, and this community."

"Should we be the ones to do this? We could just tell the authorities and they could do it." Donna says to John.

"They would have done it by now Donna. If we can put two and two together don't you think they would have done that too?" he looks at her then the rest of them.

"John's right" Vicky says, "It's upto us to finish off what they could never do. We can end their torment, and if it was me in that tunnel I would want someone to do that for me."

"You're right Vicky, come on gang let's do this for those poor people's spirits." Martin stands up and pats John on the back. "Come on mate let's get the torches and a couple of spades out the cars."

They all go outside, and they can feel the air is so clear and crisp after the storm and their spirits rise. They all get a torch and head for the tunnel service door. Martin opens the door and they step into the tunnel.

It's very dark in the tunnel so they all turn their torches on and shine them all over the tunnel. Water drips from the roof of the tunnel as it seeps through from the ground above.

They all spread out across the width of the tunnel so they don't miss anything, and the lights from their torches light the tunnel up as they walk slowly. John shines his torch down briefly and he spots the rails.

"There are still rails in here so be careful, and don't trip over them." They walk on and a couple of minutes later his torch lights up one of the trains carriages. "Here we go, here's the train." They all turn their torches towards the carriage and they stand in amazement.

"Oh my, look at the state of this carriage" Martin says as they get closer. This one is on an angle and right across the tunnel, but it seems to mostly intact.

The carriage is upright and they walk to it cautiously, in case there might be something loose that might fall on them. They check it over and slowly walk along side it till they find a way in. They find an exit door on the side and they open the door.

The door is stiff on its hinges but they get it open, and they all climb onto the carriage. This train had wooden carriages and this one is a bit twisted but undamaged. They check to see if there are any bones on this one but find none. They walk the length of the carriage and step out the far end and back onto the rails. Infront of them are two more carriages but these are badly twisted and damaged.

They walk cautiously through these two carriages, avoiding snapped wooden panels and roof beams, then their torches light up some bones. The girls stand in shock, covering their open mouths at the sight of these bones.

"Look there" Vicky says to everyone as she looks at her friends.

"It looks as if we have found our first bones." John walks past Vicky and crouches down beside the bones. He looks at the gang. "These are the bones of two children by the look and size of them."

"Let's gather them up and put them in one of the bags we brought. We must get every single bone, no matter how small." Martin says as he helps John gather the two children's bones and they gently put them into a bag.

The girls are a little squeamish, but they knew that this was going to happen, so they help by checking the carriage. They have to move smashed chairs, broken glass and wood panels to find bones.

The carriage is searched fully and all bones are gathered up before they move on. John stops the gang and they wonder why. "I think we should separate the children's bones from the adults and put them into separate bags to honour their memory. All the bones will be buried in the same grave, but it just feels right to have the children's separate, do you all agree?"

"Yeah" they all reply and they carry on searching. When the two carriages have been cleared they move on. The gang go through the other 5 carriages, gathering every last bone and fragment of bone and when they are done they feel proud.

John steps out the last carriage, the one closest to the engine, and he sees the big steam engine infront of him. It is laid on its side and covered in dust and water from the roof. He climbs onto the engine to make sure none of the carriages jumped the engine, and when he gets to the top of the engine he shines his torch. "Oh my god" he shouts and the others come out the carriage. "Come and look at this."

Vicky is the first onto the engine. "What is it dear?" she asks worried. The others soon climb onto the engine and shine their torches all-round the tunnel, and there in the lights they see something they all wasn't expecting. Laid on its side infront of them is another steam train's engine.

"I guess we now know what caused the train crash." He looks at his friends in the lights of their torches and they are all amazed.

"Well who would have guessed it eh? We all thought the old woman was the cause of the crash, but this train must have been the cause." Donna stands there looking at the other engine.

"Just out of curiosity, this train isn't a passenger train too, is it?" Sarah asks. "Only wondering, because we will need to gather all their bones too, won't we?"

"Come on Martin, let's go check it out."

"Right behind you mate." They both climb down off the engine and walk past the other overturned one and the girls watch as they disappear out of sight.

The guys pass the engine and John spots a freight carriage, and another one behind it. "This is a freight train mate."

"So there are no passenger carriages on this one?"

"No" he says to him, "but we will have to gather the driver and his stoker to bury with the rest of the victims. They deserve to be buried too, even if they caused the crash."

"You're right, they all died in the same crash and in the same tunnel, so they should all be buried together." Martin and John search the engine and find the remains of the two engine crew and gather their bones.

As they get the last few bones they hear Sarah shouting. They grab the bag and rush back to the girls. They climb over the first engine and as they do they see a white ghostly figure of a woman, floating.

The guys join the girls and they all look at the ghostly figure. The woman turns slowly and looks directly at John, and he steps back. The ghost floats down from the engine and stops infront of them all, but mostly John.

"Thank you for your help and setting us free. We have been trapped here since the crash and our spirits have not been able to roam further than this tunnel. We all thank you for doing this for us and as soon as we are laid to rest we can finally move on to the afterlife. Thank you all."

# Chapter 5

They all stand their looking at the ghostly figure in shock and surprise and the ghost disappears. The gang look at each other and the girls have a tear in their eyes.

"Come on gang, let's bury these bones and set these poor people free. The gang gather the bags of bones and walk back to the tunnel entrance. The cold, dark tunnel seems a little warmer as they walk slowly, so they don't break any of the bones, back to the entrance.

John and Martin dig the grave about twenty foot square and a couple of feet deep, and when it's done they all open the bags and gently spread the bones in the grave, making sure none of the bones touch each other.

Once the bones have been laid out, John and Martin slowly cover the bones with the soil and once the grave has been filled in the gang stand there. They all look at John.

"John we want you to say a few words for these people as it was your idea to do this." Sarah smiles and he looks at the others and they are smiling too.

"Ok" he replies. He stands close to the edge of the grave and bows his head. "We gathered here want to say a final goodbye to the victims of the 1957 train crash. We hope that your spirits can now move on and be set free from your twenty two year torment. We wish you will all be able to move on now and hope that you will remember us because we will remember you." He pauses and next to him a ghostly figure of a small girl appears and she has a smile on her face. She reaches out for John's hand and he holds it out. The little girl wraps her hand around his and John feels her soft but cold hand in his and he looks at her.

The rest of the gang are amazed and the girls have to wipe away a tear or two from their eyes as they watch. John looks down at the little girl and she has a smile on her face.

"Thank you for setting us all free. You are all caring people and now you have set us free we can go to heaven in peace. We all thank you and we will all remember you. Thank you all." She looks at the others and smiles and they all smile back to her.

As they stand there the little girl disappears and the gang stand alone in the dark tunnel. "That was awesome" Sarah says, almost crying. They stand in the tunnel, then all of a sudden there is a bright beam of light shining down from the roof, and as they all watch they see all the passengers and the train drivers and stokers going up into the light. The last one to go is the little girl, and as she ascends into the light to heaven, she waves to them all and they wave back, then she disappears and the bright beam of light goes out, leaving the gang in darkness.

The gang walk out of the tunnel into a beautiful sunny morning and they look around the old station. Unknown to them an old gentleman and his wife are crossing over the top of the tunnels bridge and they see the gang. They hear them talking about the train crash and stop to listen.

"Well my friends we set those people free from their torment and now, as we all saw, they have gone upto heaven, released from their twenty two years in that tunnel. It feels good to do something that has made a difference to others and I think we all feel the same." John says, not knowing the couple are above them.

"It was so nice to see them all going up the light to heaven, and that little girl was so cute and when she held your hand

John that was so special." Vicky hugs John and the others are almost in tears again.

"Just to satisfy my curiosity, how did that feel when she held your hand?" Martin is curious.

The old couple are intrigued at this conversation and listen on. The old lady is part of the local newspaper team and they know this would make a great piece for the paper.

"Well mate when she held my hand it felt nice but cold and soft. It was a strange feeling but good too." He looks at them all, "come on its time for us to go home."

On the bridge the couple walk down to the gang as they go to their cars and they stop them. "Excuse me, could we have a word with you please?"

The gang think they are in trouble for staying at the station so they stand and listen to the couple. "Have we done something wrong?" Donna asks them.

"We only stayed in the station because of the storm." Sarah adds.

"No it's not that" the man says and he goes over to John. "We heard what you said about the train crash and setting those people free from their torment. We are part of the local paper and we would be interested in your story for our paper. We would pay you of course . . ."

John stops them in mid-sentence. "We would be happy to share our story, but as for payment we would prefer if you could set up a memorial for those poor victims."

"That sound really good" the old lady says, "and very thoughtful." She looks at them all. "What sort of memorial would you suggest?"

"Well I think the best one would be to restore this station and have your news reports up on the walls and of course all the old newspaper reports about the crash. There are lots in the waiting room on the table. Would you all agree on that gang?"

"Oh yes that would be good" they all say.

"That is so thoughtful of you all" the old lady says to them all. "We can get that done for you."

The gang tell them all the details and they write it down and when they have finished the gang shake their hands and the couple leave.

Vicky looks at John. "That was a nice gesture John, and having the station restored in their honour and memory was a nice touch."

"Yeah that was a good idea, those people will like that." Sarah looks at John and then goes over to him and gives him a hug. Vicky looks on but she's not worried.

"Well gang time for us to leave. Our work here is done." They all get in their cars and slowly they leave the old station. They all take one last look at the station and drive away.

Time passes and the gang decide to visit the old station to see if the old couple's promise of restoration has been done. The gang pull up in the stations car park and they can see the station has been fully restored and there are several cars in the car park.

The old couple see them pull up and they rush out to meet them. The gang see them, big smiles on their faces and they rush to the gang and shake all their hands.

"Welcome back to the station" the old lady says with a big smile on her face.

"As you can see the station has been fully restored and we have put lots of the news reports all around the station walls.

The gang follow them into the waiting room and they look around. The walls have been painted in the stations original colours and there are posters all around. The gang look around as other people are doing the same. They feel so proud and know that this is a fitting tribute to all the crash victims.

The tunnel has been totally sealed off at both ends so no one can disturb the trains and the rails have been replaced alongside the platform. John sees the rails and wonders why they have put them back.

"Sir, can I ask you something please?"

"Certainly John, whats on your mind?" the old man asks him.

"Why have the rails been put back alongside the platform?"

"Ah glad you asked me that. Can you all come with me please." The gang are curious and follow him onto the platform. They stand at the edge, just where the dark figured lady jumped off the platform.

"The reason we replaced the rails is because we are getting a replica set of carriages to put alongside the platform in those peoples memory. They will be exact replicas of their carriages and all funds raised will be used to keep the station clean and tidy."

"That's wonderful" Sarah says.

"What a good idea." Donna says to the man.

"Well we thought so too young lady. This station has been derelict since the crash, and now this will let everyone know what happened here." The old man shakes their hands again, and they head back to the waiting room. The gang have a cup of coffee and something to eat from the restored kitchen and go round reading all the news reports.

The End

# The Derelict

# Chapter 1

———❦·◆·❦———

The Deep Star is a Stella ship, a huge deep space Stella mapping ship, sent out in 2017 to map the known universe so we humans can have a map to use for space trade routes to planets, moons or other solar systems wishing to trade with Earth.

The Deep Star is a huge ship about 2 miles long and has a crew of over a thousand. The ship left our solar system in 2019 and was never heard from again.

It is now 2075 and trade routes have been made to many planets and star systems and alien races from far off solar systems and planets trade with our planet. Earth has become popular for its trade in minerals, ore and synthetic water.

Earth makes machinery for planets to extract water from various elements in their atmospheres, and alien races come from far and wide.

Earth also has a huge reputation for salvage and in space harbours around the planet the salvaged wreckage of old or destroyed starships are used for repairing damaged starships, or to build buildings on planets and moons.

Harbour one is the most productive salvage team around the planet, and they have a very good reputation. They are all good at their jobs, but they do rely on the salvage ships to bring quality salvage back, and the most famous salvage ship of all is the Orion.

The Orion is one of the harbours biggest salvage ships and has travelled to many star systems, and for most alien races, this is the ship they all call for if there is any salvage they cannot handle. The Orion crew go in, strip the ship or whatever they have been called in for then sell it back to the alien race at a reasonable profit.

This has proved very popular among a lot of alien races and star systems, so there is usually a lot of work for them.

The Captain of the Orion is a 50yr old man called Drake. He has been in the salvage business since the age of 20, and he knows everything there is to know about all salvage, and especially starships. He and his crew can strip an average sized starship in a matter of months, and this is why they are in big demand.

Drake has heard of the Deep Star and was shocked when they never returned from their mission, and he has always wondered what happened to them. His best friend, a man called John Geller, was the Captain of the Deep Star, and he wondered if he would ever see him again, but when he found out the ship had vanished, his hope of seeing his friend again vanished too.

Drake and his crew have just returned from the Alycian star system and he and his crew are having a well-earned rest, after netting themselves 700,000 credits, each. The rest of his crew are away at bars or with their families enjoying themselves.

Drake is checking his ship over, as he normally does, and he sits in his chair on the darkened bridge, and he sips a cup of Jovian coffee. The light's from various monitors and console's light up the bridge in a mellow glow.

Drake relaxes in his chair and he looks out the bridge main window at the vast emptiness of space, which he loves to travel through. Drake isn't married and he is not in any relationship because he loves not having any ties.

Drake is in a world of his own, dreaming of salvage when his personal console comes on. He looks at the screen and there, on the screen, is the commander of Harbour one, Darren Robson. Drake is Robson's number 1 salvage man.

"Drake" he says smiling, "I have some news for you."

"What news is that then?" he replies with no facial expression at all.

"Oh I think this will interest you Drake" he says, looking striaght at the screen.

"Go on then, tell me what this great news is." Drake sips his coffee, still relaxed.

"You remember the Deep Star, don't you Drake?"

Drake leans forward. "Yes I do" he says stirring at the screen, "Why?"

"Well the ship has been seen in the Cylanian system" he looks at Drake open eyed. Drake leans on the arm of his chair, interested now.

"Really" he answers Robson. "Is she on her way home to Earth?"

"Not exactly, Drake" Robson replies. Robson looks at Drake with a look of worry on his face and Drake looks at him puzzled.

"What do you mean by that, Robson?" Drake enquires.

"Well from the report we got, the Deep Star is dead in space, and from the alien race that found her they tell us the ship looks as if it has been in a battle and the ship is severely damaged."

"So do you want us to go and check her out?" Drake is hopeful, and hope's he says yes.

"Sure do Drake. You can leave when you're ready" he looks at Drake, "oh and if you can bring her back to port, I reckon you will get a massive salvage fee, because the owners of the ship have long since thought the ship had been destroyed and so destroyed all their documentation on her, so she is now free salvage." He looks at Drake and knows he will be interested in this, knowing he knew the captain of this ship. "So are you interested Drake?"

"You bet I am, I'll call my crew back and let you know when we are ready to go."

Drake gets on his com link and contacts all his crew and after a few course remarks and jokes from them, they all agree to return to the Orion.

An hour later the last of the crew members has returned and all are on board the Orion. Drake gathers them on the bridge, and all 16 crew members wait for an explanation.

"I've called you all back because I have some startling news to tell you all. While you were all off enjoying yourselves, I got some really good news." He looks at his crew and they all look puzzled. "I assume you have all heard of the Stella mapping ship, Deep Star?"

They look at Drake astonished, and they all reply at once, "Yeah" they say out loud. His 1st officer, Denver, looks at Drake.

"What about the Deep Star Captain?" he asks him.

"Well the ship has been found in the Cylanian system, and from the alien race that spotted her, they told Robson she was dead in space and they also said it looks as if she had been attacked. We have had permission to go and bring her back as salvage"

"So what kind of salvage are we looking at here cap?" Finch asks Drake.

"Free salvage Finch" he says to him, "we have full rights to her, and if we can bring her back to Harbour 1, we'll get the full salvage price for her." He looks at his crew and their facial expressions say it all. "That means we will be in for the biggest salvage ever."

"How much then, cap?" Finch asks excited now.

"Ten million credits Finch" he looks at them all and they cheer.

"Ten million, wow that's what I call a good salvage cap." Finch replies. Drake calms his crew down and they stand quiet.

"Ah bear in mind that we have to bring her back in one piece, if we can."

"One piece cap, that's a tall order. If this ship has been attacked, who knows what damage has been done, and most importantly, the control systems might be damaged or non-functional."

"I know that the control systems could be out of order, but we are a good salvage team and we have seen a lot of damaged ships in our time, but we can get this ship going again." He looks at his crew and they all look eager to get started. "Let's go get us a Stella starship."

His crew cheer and those not working on the bridge leave, and return to their own jobs. Drake sits in his chair and looks out the main window. He turns to his helmsmen, Lucas and Sharp, and smiles.

"Lucas, plot a course for the Cylanian system please" and he looks over to his 1st officer, stood close by. Denver smile's and Drake turns to his helmsman.

"Course set Captain" Lucas replies.

"Thank you Lucas" he says then looks at Sharp. "Sharp, punch it."

"Yes Captain" he says and he presses several buttons and the ship begins to move slowly.

"Sharp, when we clear the port, jump us to hyperspace."

"Yes captain."

The Orion moves away from harbour 1, and when the ship has cleared the port, Sharp jumps the ship into hyperspace. The Cylanian system is over a million light years away and it will take around 4 hours to get there, then they have to find the Deep Star.

# Chapter 2

The Cylanian system is made up of ten planets and one sun. The largest planet is called Yelvik, and is about the size of Jupiter, but this planet is no gas giant, but solid rock, like Earth.

The Deep Star is on the far side of Yelvik, in a stable orbit. Yelvik has 4 moons and the largest is about the size of Titan. The alien race who discovered the Deep Star live on the smallest planet in the system, Mex. They spotted the ship on a routine trade route to Lon, the 2$^{nd}$ largest planet, and they said it just appeared overnight.

The Orion speeds through hyperspace towards the Cylanian system, and on the bridge, Drake sits in his chair. "How long till we get to the Cylanian system, Lucas?" he looks over to him and Lucas checks his data.

"About another hour captain" he says. Drake looks over to his comms officer, Wilson.

"Wilson, are there any communications coming through about the Deep Star?"

"No sir, it's all quiet at the moment."

"Patch me through to Robson on harbour 1." Wilson opens a link and gets Robson on the star link. "Sir, Robson is on the link."

"Thanks Wilson" and Drake open's his link on his chair control. He sees Robson on his screen. "Robson, we are about an hour away from the Cylanian system and we need to know which planet the Deep Star is in orbit around."

"You're in luck Drake, we just had the Krellon's on the space link, and they have told me the Deep Star is in a stable orbit around Yelvik, the largest planet."

"Yelvik you say, good, I'll get Lucas to plot a course for that planet when we come out of hyperspace."

Robson looks at Drake on his screen with some concern. "Be careful Drake, the ship has been missing for years, and we don't know what has gone on with that ship. If it has been attacked then the aliens who did it could still be on board."

Drake smiles at Robson. "Didn't know you cared, Robson" he says sarcastically. "Don't worry about us we've been on plenty of deserted and damaged ships, so we know what to look for, and what to look out for."

"Well just be careful Drake" he looks at him on his screen, "I'll leave it in your hands." Robson knows he can't win any arguments with Drake.

Drake looks out the main bridge window then looks down towards Lucas and Sharp. "Sharp, do we have a system map for the Cylanian System?"

"Er . . . yes Captain" he checks the data banks and finds it, "I'll put it on the window viewer sir." The window viewer on the Orion has a double use function, the first is that it is the bridge view out to the stars, and second is that any information they need to see can be super imposed onto the window.

The Cylanian system map comes on the window with all the planets and moons and their descriptions. Drake looks at the map and he sees all the planets, moons and the suns position on the viewer. He stirs at the map for several seconds then he turns to his helmsmen.

"Sharp, which planet is Yelvik?" Put it up on the left image viewer please."

"Yes Captain" and he gathers the data then puts it on the left image viewer, which is part of the main window too, and the planet Yelvik comes on in high detail, and beside the planets picture all the relevant information about the planet is also displayed.

The viewer also has a right image viewer, and this one is mainly used to display orbital paths of planets and moons.

Drake goes over to look closer at the system map and as he stirs at the map, his bridge crew look on. Lucas gets a warning buzzer on his console display and he looks down to see what it is.

"Captain, we are closing in on the Cylanian system" Lucas says out loud so Drake can hear him.

"Drop us out of hyperspace, and plot our course to Yelvik" Drake says without turning round.

"Yes Captain" Lucas replies and he and Sharp start the sub light sequence. The Orion slows to sub light speed and comes out of hyperspace on the edge of the Cylanian system. Lucas plots the course to Yelvik and looks over to Drake.

"Course plotted to Yelvik Captain."

"Good" Drake says then turns round and walks back to his chair. "Punch it, Sharp."

"Yes Captain." Sharp hits the controls and the ship turns slightly and moves slowly through the system. The main map has been turned off so they can all see the system as they pass through it. The crew of the Orion have never been to this system before, so they don't know which planet they want.

"Which one is Mex, Lucas? Put it on the main viewer please."

"Hang on sir and I'll find it." He punches in some commands and the planet comes on the left image viewer.

Denver walks over to Drake. "Captain, I thought we were heading for Yelvik?"

"We are Denver, but the aliens who discovered the Deep Star live on Mex. I just wanted to know which planet it was, so we can thank them later."

"Oh" Denver says and Drake pats him on his shoulder and smiles. Drake goes and sits in his chair.

"Wilson, get me Knox on the com please."

"Right sir" and he gets Knox, the ships chief engineer, on the com.

"Knox here Captain, what can I do for you?"

"When we get on the Deep Star I want you and some of your crew to find out why she's dead in space."

"You can count on us Captain, we'll find out why." Knox pauses and Drake realises the link is still open, and he knows Knox has more to say. "Captain, did you say the Deep Star?"

"Yes Knox, why do you ask?" Drake is curious now.

"Didn't that ship disappear in 2019 sir?"

"It did, and now it has re-appeared, and we are almost there."

"You can count on us to do our best and get her moving again sir." Knox and his crew are the best there is.

"Good man, Drake out." Wilson closes the com and Drake looks out the main window at this beautiful system.

The Orion passes the two outer planets and then they come up on Mex, the Krellon's home. Denver has been monitoring the Orion's flight path, and he sees they are approaching Mex, so he goes over to Drake, who is looking out the main window.

"Captain, we are approaching Mex" and he points it out to Drake.

"So that's Mex is it?" he says looking at the small planet. "Not a bad looking planet, as planets go."

# Chapter 3

————⟫•◦•⟪————

Mex is the smallest planet in the system, but its rich in Crystal Ice, a useful mineral for fuelling their starships and power stations. The Krellon are a small race of aliens, about the size of a 7-8yr old Earth child, but they are hard workers and they trade their Crystal Ice throughout the system.

The Orion passes Mex and the next planet is Yelvik, the one they are after, so Drake and Denver stand at the window looking at this beautiful planet.

Drake goes back to his chair and sits down. He reads the data about the planet on the main image viewer, and he reads that the planet is far enough from the sun to sustain life, but as far as everyone knows, no life has ever been found on Yelvik.

"Lucas, have you spotted the Deep Star yet? She is in a stable orbit around this planet somewhere, so when you find her let me know."

"Yes Captain, I'll do that." Lucas starts a scan of the planet to find the ship.

Drake and Denver look at Yelvik as they close in on it, and they can see that it looks a lot like Earth, but just on a bigger scale. As the Orion glides past the planet, they see the sun glinting off the water on the planet's surface. They see land masses, rivers, mountains and clouds in the atmosphere, and it reminds them both of Earth.

Lucas calls to Drake. "Captain, I've found the Deep Star, she is about 5 miles from our current position."

"Thanks Lucas" he says to his helmsman. He looks at Sharp. "Plot a course for that ship."

"Yes Captain" and he does it, "course plotted sir." He has put the position of the Orion, the Deep Star and the projected path on the image viewer and Drake and Denver study it carefully.

Drake turns to his 1st officer. "Well here we go, we've found her." He looks at Denver, "I want you to arm a party of the crew and when we reach the Deep Star we'll go on board and find out what happened to here."

"Ok Captain" he says and starts to walk away, then turns back. "Who's going sir?"

"We will need Knox and some of his engineers and get Black, Henson, Finch, Hedges, Hill and Grant. We need to leave a party of the crew on board the Orion, just incase there is an emergency." Drake looks at Denver, and he nods in confirmation.

"I'll go and get our crystal laser guns and arm those that are going." Denver starts to walk away again, and Drake stops him.

"Oh and we'll need Davis, our medic, to go with us incase there are any survivors" and Drake looks at him again, "oh and us two of course."

"I'll get the laser guns and hand them out, and I'll get Knox to prepare the Astro—Suits." Denver leaves the bridge and Drake turns to his bridge crew and walks back to his chair but stops at his helmsmen consoles.

"Lucas, Sharp I want you to monitor us on the Astro-suit monitors and I want to know how everyone is doing and if you think something is wrong with anyone, including me, then you let me know, Ok?"

"Yes Captain" they both say together.

Drake looks over to his comms operator, Wilson. "Wilson, I want you tom keep the link from our suits to the ship open at all times, incase we need to leave . . . quickly."

"Will do sir" he replies and he sits in his chair and prepares the Astro-suit special link, and he knows this is a big responsibility he's been given.

Drake walks over to the one crewman who hasn't said much and has had his nose buried in his computer. He stops near his science officer, and taps him on the shoulder.

"Scott, you haven't had much to say on this journey." Scott turns to Drake and looks at his Captain.

"I know Captain, but I have been checking out this planet, and it has some remarkable qualities sir." He looks at Drake with a look of excitement.

"Such as what?" Drake is interested in any opinion of any of his crew.

"There is a high concentration of gold, silver and phelon crystals down there sir. There is also a vast amount of other high grade minerals, and I also found Dextron, a super and light mineral."

"Dextron you say, interesting. When we have got the Deep Star up and running we will go down to the planet's surface and gather some of these minerals and of course the gold and silver eh?" Drake looks at Scott with a smile on his face. "You locate the best sources and we'll go later."

"I'll do that Captain, and for now I'll keep it to myself."

"Best way, we don't want the crew to get strange ideas, or I'll have to lay my law down, and you know what that means eh?"

"Everyone knows your law Captain, and if they have any sense they would never cross you." Scott knows what his temper is like, because he has seen him in action.

"You got that right, Scott." Drake walks away from Scott and he walks over to the main window to look out on the planet below. He stands there for a couple of minutes then he suddenly realises that he doesn't know what Dextron is. He goes back to Scott.

"Scott, what is Dextron, I've never heard of that mineral before."

"It's a crystallised form of liquid fuel, used for fuelling starships, but its qualities make it more efficient at making the fuel go further, and this stuff would bring us a big profit back on Earth."

"Sounds good to me, Scott, but keep this information just between us till we come back from the Deep Star Ok? This will be a bit extra for the crew to look forward to eh?"

"No problem Captain, I'll tell no one." Drake pats him on his shoulder and walks off to his chair. As he is walking to his chair, Lucas stops him.

"Captain we are coming up on the Deep Star." Drake looks at him with a smile.

"Great" he says to him and Drake walks over to the main window and waits.

The Orion closes in on the Deep Star and Drake looks at the ship as they slowly approach it. As the Orion passes the ship, Drake can see a lot of damage and he can't see what may have caused it, but he has an idea it wasn't a meteor or something natural, but more than likely another ship.

The Orion slows down as they come upon an airlock, and Sharp slows their ship and as they get alongside the airlock, Drake sees a gaping hole down the side of the Deep Star.

"Good god, look at that," he says tom his bridge crew and they all look.

"Wonder what caused that sir" Lucas asks Drake.

"I have no idea Lucas, but at a guess it could be anything from an internal blast to a meteor hit."

"It would have to have been a bloody big one Captain, that hole has to be about half a mile long." Lucas stirs at the gaping hole and he can see some of the ships internal structure.

"I just hope the ships log has recorded it all then we can know for sure." Drake looks at the hole and he knows this was not a meteor strike, but he keeps it to himself.

The Orion pulls alongside the airlock and Sharp manoeuvres the ship to the airlock docking clamps, and when they are docked, he looks at Drake.

"Captain, we are docked."

"Good, well done Sharp." He goes over to Scott. "Scott can you get any sort of reading's about the atmosphere inside the ship?"

"Hold on sir, I'll run a scan." Scott starts an internal scan of the Deep Star, and gets the results quickly. "It seems there is some air on that ship, but it's too weak for us to breathe."

"Thanks Scott." Drake goes over to his comms operator. "Wilson, get me Freeman would you, please."

Wilson gets on the comm to Freeman, the salvage deck commander. "Freeman is on the com sir."

"Commander Freeman, Drake here. Could you prepare the Astro-suits for 15 crew members please."

"No problem Captain, I'll get right on it."

"Thank you, Drake out." Drake looks over to Lucas. "Lucas, put the ships display on the centre screen on the main window please. I want an internal scan of the ship showing all the decks, crews quarters, engine rooms and bridge location from our present position at this airlock."

"Yes sir" Lucas says as he puts the ships display on the main window. Several seconds later the outline of the ship, and all the decks and quarters are shown, along with the engine rooms location, super imposed on the window.

Drake walks over to the window viewer and takes a good look at the Deep Star's internal structure. He and his crew can see this ship has a lot of decks then he spots the bridge, and points to it.

"This is where we need to get to. Can you plot a route from here to the bridge, Lucas?" he looks at Lucas.

"Way ahead of you on that, Captain" Lucas says and he brings the quickest route up on the display.

Drake looks at the route and from their airlock and it's only 5 decks up to the bridge. "Wilson, get the team up here. I want them to study this plan so they know what they are up against."

"Ok Captain" Wilson says. He contacts all the team Drake has asked for, and they all acknowledge him. Wilson looks at Drake, who is still studying the Deep Star's plan. "All on their way up now, captain."

"Good" he says without turning round. A few minutes later the team arrive on the bridge and Drake turns round to face them. "Ok, this is the Deep Star's internal plan. Study it carefully so you know where you need to go. Don't be too worried, I'll have all this information put through into the Astro-suits, so you won't be totally in the dark."

The team study the plan of the ship and Drake looks at them as they do. "One more thing" he says and they turn round, "this ship is dead in space, so it's possible that there are no lights still working, so we will all be in the darkness, but the suits have lights on them, so please use them Ok."

"Ok Captain" they all say, confirming his order.

"Let's suit up" Drake says as he starts to walk off the bridge the others follow him. They go down to the salvage bay and put their Astro-suits on. Each crew member has their own suit, and they get them on and are ready to go. Drake leads them to the airlock and they enter.

Freeman locks the door behind them, and Drake opens the outer door and there is a hiss as the pressure equalises, and they walk forward. They walk slowly to the Deep Star's airlock door, and they are all a bit nervous at what they might see when the door is opened, but they are trained men and women and have done this plenty of times before, and the nervous feeling soon goes.

Drake opens the airlock on the Deep Star and there is a hiss as the pressure equalises, and they walk onto the Deep Star. The ship is dark and cold and in their suit lights they can all see the ship walls and deck are covered in a deep frost.

They all walk forward and Drake closes the airlock, and they are all alone on the ship. They walk forward a few metres and come out in the cargo bay area. They all turn in different directions to look round the bay and frost covers everything.

"Ok use your tracking monitors to find where you need to be. Knox, I want you to go to engineering and see if you can get us some heat and light in here." Drake looks at his team and Knox nods his head in acknowledgement.

"Yes Captain" he replies, and he takes 5 of his engineers, and they walk away.

"The rest of you spread out and see if you can find any evidence of what happened here." Drake says as he checks his tracking monitor for the route to the bridge.

"Yes Captain" they reply.

"Denver, Davis and Grant, you follow me to the bridge." Drake and his small team set off towards the bridge, using the tracking monitor to guide their way.

# Chapter 4

———❧•○•☙———

D rake and his team go up 5 decks and soon see the doors
to the bridge. The doors are slightly open so Drake and
Denver prise them open, and they all walk onto the bridge.

The 4 of them look around and the bridge is lit by the
planets glow, but this is enough for them to see.

Knox and his crew reach the engineering section and as
they check the panels, they can see that all the systems have
been turned off. Knox turns to his crew.

"That's very strange" he says looking at his crew. "Why is
everything turned off, and not run down?"

"No idea sir" Clark says, "but I've found the main power
switch."

"Good man Clark" Knox says patting him on the back,
"turn it on and let's see what happens."

Clark pushes the lever up till it makes contact, but nothing happens. Knox looks at him. "Try it again Clark" and he does. This time the lights on the deck flicker several times and they hear the power generators start up, and seconds later the lights come on.

All over the ship the lights come on and the Deep Star is slowly coming back to life. On the bridge Drake and his team are amazed to see the light come on. Drake tries the ships intercom.

"Hope you can hear me Knox, well done to you and your crew. I knew you wouldn't let me down."

"Thank you Captain" comes the reply over the intercom.

"Are the heat generators working aswell?" Drake is pleased with his crews.

"Yes sir but it will take a good hour before the ship is back upto temperature."

"Glad to hear that, Knox. Keep up the good work." Drake looks at his team as they stand on the bridge, looking at all the computer consoles, but none of them have come on.

The rest of the boarding party have split up and are checking out the rest of the ship. Everyone knows that no one could have survived the coldness of the ship, but they want to find the crew so they can return them to Earth for a proper burial.

On the bridge, Drake and his team turn on all the consoles, and most of them come to life, but some have broken screens and there are splatters of blood on them.

They all look round the bridge, then Grant lets out a scream as she spots something. Denver and Drake look at her. "What is I Grant?" Drake asks her as they walk over to her.

She points down to the side of one of the consoles. "Look sir" she says, nearly vomiting. They look down to where she is pointing and they see the chewed remains of a human arm.

"Bloody hell" Drake says out loud, and he bends down for a closer look. He looks it over then spots a tattoo on the arm, and he knows who the arm belonged to. The arm is from his good friend and the Captain of the Deep Star, John Geller. "It's John Geller's arm" he says looking at Denver and Grant.

"Who was he sir?" Grant enquires.

"He was the Captain of the Deep Star and my good friend."

"Sorry about that Captain" Grant says in a soft voice, patting his shoulder.

"That's Ok Grant." Drake is puzzled at the chewed remains and he looks at the other 2 of his team. "What the hell happened on this ship? And more to the point, where are the rest of the crew?"

Down in engineering, Knox and his crew are getting the heaters on and suddenly something runs across the bay, very fast, and disappears through the open door.

"What the hell was that" he says and his crew look bewildered.

"I never got a good look at it sir, but it was big and fast." Clark looks at everyone and they all look at the door.

"Could it have been one of the crew chief?" Telford says nervously.

"Believe me Telford, that was no crew member, it was too big."

"If it's not a crew member, then what was it?" Clark is getting nervous now.

"I have no idea, but I'll have to inform Drake about this." Knox opens the intercom to Drake's suit. "Captain this is Knox here."

On the bridge Drake is still checking out the arm. "What is it Knox?" he enquires.

"Sir we aren't alone on this ship." Drake is stunned by the message and he stands up. Denver and Grant look at him.

"Anything wrong Captain?" Grant asks, but Drake holds his arm up to keep her quiet.

"What do you mean Knox, not alone?"

"I mean there is something else onboard this ship, other than us sir." Denver and Grant are worried now and Drake goes over to a nearby chair and sits down.

"Are you sure, Knox?" he asks interested now, and he looks at the other 2 of his team. "What did you see?"

"Not really sure sir, but it wasn't one of our crew. It was too big and very fast sir." Drake senses fear in his voice.

"Put your gun on stun Knox and go and see if you can find it, then stun it and report back to me."

"Right Captain" Knox replies and the link goes off. The engineers all set their laser guns to stun and they cautiously walk to the open door, and slowly go into the corridor.

On the bridge Drake has told Denver and Grant what Knox reported and so they set about checking the ships data banks for any clues.

Grant comes across the ships travel log and she calls Drake over. "Captain look at this" she says excited.

"What have you found Grant?"

"It's the flight log sir" she says as he stands next to her. "I'll run the log from the last entry." She presses several buttons on the console and the flight log begins. They all watch and the log shows where the ship has been.

They see star systems far and wide and see visual displays of planets, moons and suns and galaxies of all shapes and sizes then they see another ship.

Drake stops the log and zooms in on the ship. The ship is black, no visual markings and its right ahead of the Deep Star just as the bridge viewer recorded it.

The ship is silhouetted by a green planet, and as they watch the log, they see the ship fire on the Deep Star then the log goes off. They all look at each other and then back to the blank screen.

"Now we know what happened" he says looking at Grant and Denver. "The ship was attacked and in my vast years of space travel I have never seen a ship like that."

"Wonder who they are?" Denver says to the others.

"One thing still puzzles me Captain" she says looking at Drake, "according to the co-ordinates on here, this happened 2 million light years away, so how did the Deep Star get here?"

Drake and Denver look at her and they are both puzzled too. "Good question Grant" he says to her.

"Perhaps some of the crew survived the attack and tried to get the Deep Star back to Earth." Denver says out loud.

"So why did they stop here?" Grant enquires. Drake looks around the bridge and then a horrible thought crosses his mind.

"Oh hell" he shouts and starts to walk off the bridge.

"What is it Captain?" Denver asks him, and Drake turns to them both.

"A thought has just occurred to me and it's not a nice one either." Drake sits in the captain's chair and opens the captain's log. "Let's see if my friend John can shine a light on this mystery."

Drake puts the log onto the main viewer and they all watch as John Geller's image come on the viewer.

They all watch and listen as John goes through several logs, then he comes to the one where the ship was attacked. This is part of that log..

"The ship has encountered what seems to be a derelict ship, hanging in orbit around a planet called Colesyn. We scanned the ship for any signs of life, but according to our scanners the ship was devoid of life. Our scanners also found no damage to the hull of the derelict ship." Drake and his crew watch, then they see the ship open fire on the Deep Star, and they see John come back to the screen log. "Oh my god" he starts shouting, while in the background they can all hear screams from the crew. Geller's voice comes on again.

"The ship has fired on us again and they have taken out the gravity generators, and we are losing our life support systems and we are . . ." the log stops, and Drake, Denver and Grant all look at each other in shock.

# Chapter 5

In the engineering bay, Knox and his crew are cautiously going from bay to bay, trying to track down what they saw. They split into 2 teams and they search a bay, moving slowly and checking every nook and cranny for the creature.

Knox and two of his crew go through a door into the life support generator room, while the other 3 crew members search the fuel bay.

Knox and his team check their bay slowly and they soon find the damage to the life support generators, then they hear a blood curdling scream.

"What the hell was that?" Knox says to his team. They all look at him, scared now. "Come on, let's check it out." They all run down the corridor to the fuel bay and they go in slow and cautiously, and as they pass the arch Knox sees blood, and lots of it, on the floor infront of them.

"Oh my" Phillips says, nearly vomiting.

"Careful you two be cautious." They all walk slowly, looking round the fuel bay with their suit lights. They pass one of the fuel containers, following the blood stained floor, then they stop as they see one arm and part of a leg from one of their crew.

"Who was it Captain?" asks Phillips.

He checks the name on the arm of the suit. "It was Telford" he says looking at them.

"Oh shit" Clark says then they hear a noise just ahead. They raise their guns and wait. Travis and Holland emerge from behind another fuel container, and this makes Knox, Clark and Phillips jump. Knox walks over to them, followed by Clark and Phillips.

"God" Knox says, "You made me jump there" he says holding his chest as his heart races with fear.

"Sorry sir but when that thing got Telford we dived for cover." Travis looks at them, fear in his eyes.

"What happened here Travis?" Knox needs answers and fast.

"It came from nowhere sir, fast as light, and grabbed Telford and dragged him over the fuel containers. We heard him scream, then there was silence, then this part of his arm and leg just fell off the fuel container." He is shaking now, and Knox notices this.

"Calm down Travis" he says patting him on his arm, and Knox looks at Holland, who isn't looking too good. "Are you Ok Holland?"

"Just about sir" he says as he slows his breathing to a steady rate.

"Did you get a good look at it you two? Could you describe it?" Knox looks at Travis and Holland, hoping they did see the creature.

"No sir, it was too fast." Travis says as he calms down.

"I only know this thing is very fast and big, and judging by what has happened, hungry too sir" Holland adds.

"Ok spread out and be on guard." They all spread out around the fuel bay, and after a long search, they find no trace of the creature or the rest of Telford. "I'll inform Drake of this new development, he'll want to know about this." He turns his suits intercom on and gets hold of Drake. "Captain, this is Knox."

"What is it now, Knox" Drake says, still sat in the captain's chair on the bridge.

"One of my crew has just been killed by this bloody alien creature, sir."

Drake is stunned by this news. "What" he shouts out, and Denver and Grant look at him. "Who was it?"

"It's Telford sir. We found part of his leg and one arm after hearing a scream from the fuel bay. Travis and Holland never saw the alien sir, but they said it was big and very fast."

"Ok Knox we're on our way down to you, just wait there and be careful." He looks at his team and he remembers what he wanted to ask Knox. "Oh by the way, is the heat and oxygen back on yet?"

"Yes Captain, sorry for not telling you but . . ." Drake stops him mid sentence.

"No matter Knox, I know why. Stay there, we'll be right down." Drake turns his intercom off and gets up. He looks at Denver and Grant. "The oxygen and heat are back on, so we can remove our suits." They take their suits off and leave them on the bridge. Knox also informs the rest of the crews that the y can take their suits off, so they do.

Drake and his team make their way to Knox and his crew, made easier now the ships lifts are working.

Knox and his crews are waiting and are all sat on old fuel containers when Holland hears a noise. "Did you hear that?" he says looking round, and they all look round, but see nothing.

"There's nothing there Holland, your just jittery." Knox tries to calm him down, then from nowhere the alien appears, and they all jump to their feet, and start firing their laser guns at it.

The alien is quick and dodges the laser fire and runs around the fuel bay, quick as a flash. They all fire in different directions, hoping to hit this alien, but it's too fast for them to hit. The alien runs round and grabs Holland, and drags him off, screaming. Knox and his crew are stunned, then Drake and his team appear, and Drake notices they are on edge. "Whats up Knox?" he asks him.

"The alien just got Holland sir." he says looking all round the fuel bay, his finger on the trigger of his gun.

"Which way did it go, Knox?"

"This way Captain, follow me." As they are about to leave, the rest of the crew turn up, and now there are plenty of new hands and eyes to find this alien creature.

The full crew head off in the direction the alien went, and they move slowly and in line, with the rear person covering the rear of the team. The fuel bay has many hiding places, and all of them have to be checked.

Drake splits the crew up into 2 teams and they spread out across the fuel bay. They search all the dark and closed in places with caution then Phillips comes across the body of Holland, or what's left of him.

"Captain, over here sir." he stands in one corner next to one of the fuel injection chambers and he starts to vomit.

"What is it Phillips?" he walks over to him, followed by several of his team, and Phillips points down. Drake sees the remains of Holland. "Ah, that's a mess."

The rest of the crew come to have a look and when they see the state his body is in most of them vomit. Holland's head has been bitten in half and the remains of his brains are spread out in a pool of blood. His body has huge chunks bitten out of it, and down his back they can all see his spine has been snapped, like a twig and partially ripped out. There is a lot of blood around the body, and Davis, the medical officer comes over to examine the body.

"Good god what a mess" he says as he begins his examination. "What the hell could do something like this sir?"

Drake is lost for words. "I have no idea Davis" he looks at him and then looks round the bay. He turns back to Davis. "Do your examination and let me know the results, although it is pretty obvious how he died."

"Leave this to me sir. I'll check the body over for any parasites or strange things . . . just in case." Drake nods to him in agreement and the rest of them continue their search of the bay.

Clark goes over to Drake, a worried look on his face. "Sir that alien is still out there, somewhere, and we should find it quickly before it attacks again."

"I know Clark, but this thing is fast and the Deep Star is a big ship. We need to trap it somehow, and then we can deal with it." They all look at him and hope he has a plan.

"Any ideas on how we do that sir?" Finch asks him. He is scared but so are all the others, but Drake is their Captain, and they hope he knows what he's doing.

"No" he says abruptly, "but we have to think of a way, and soon. I don't want to lose any more of you." Drake walks away, followed by Denver, and they stop a few metres from the main door.

"I know this isn't going to be easy sir, but we need a plan, and soon. This alien must be hiding somewhere and all we have to do is find out where." Denver is concerned, and it shows.

"I'll think of something Denver, don't worry. Let's go to the bridge and check the ships internal structure for somewhere we can trap it." Drake tells the crew what he's going to do, and some decide to go with him. Drake turns to Knox. "Knox, do you think you could get this ship moving?"

"Yes sir, the engines are all in good order, and there's plenty of fuel on board." He looks at Drake, who has a small smile on his face. "Leave it to Captain."

"Good man" he says as he and some others leave the fuel bay. They walk slowly to the nearest lift, watching out for the alien as they go.

Knox, Phillips, Travis, Black and Hedges all return to the engineering section to get the ship fired up and moving. They move through the corridors slowly, checking any open doorways for the alien.

Denver, Clark, Grant, Henson, Finch and Hill all follow Drake to the bridge and Davis follows on after he has examined the body of Holland.

# Chapter 6

———————————

B ack on the space port Harbour 1, Robson has not heard from Drake or his crew for some time and he is a little worried, so he contacts the Orion. On the bridge Wilson picks up the incoming call.

"This is Robson to the Orion, do you read me, over."

Wilson answers him. "This is the Orion sir, Wilson here."

"Ah Wilson is Drake on the Deep Star yet?"

"Yes sir, they went about 2 hours ago. The Deep Star is all lit up so I can assume the ship still has power, but we haven't heard from anyone since they left the Orion sir." Wilson looks at the others on the bridge and they just shrug their shoulders.

"Please don't disturb them this is just a quick call to see if everything is Ok."

"All seems fine upto now sir, but if anything changes, I'll let you know."

"Thanks Wilson, Robson out." The link goes off and Wilson looks round at the others then continues monitoring the Deep Star.

"He gets so nervous about us" he says laughing then Drake comes on the vid link.

"Wilson this is Drake, how's everything over there?"

"All fine here Captain. We just had Robson on the comms, asking if all was Ok."

"Well it's not Wilson. We have lost Telford and Holland to a vicious alien over here." Wilson and the crew are shocked at the news.

"Are the rest of you all Ok sir?"

"We're fine Wilson. Knox is down in engineering to see if we can get the ship moving, and we are going to try and trap this alien and eject it into space. I just hope there is only one of these bloody creatures on board." Wilson is amazed at Drake's calmness.

"How do you plan to do that sir?"

"We're working on that right now." Drake looks directly at Wilson and he knows Drake has something on his mind. "If it all goes pear shaped over here, you are to separate and destroy the Deep Star to stop it getting back to Earth." He looks at Wilson. "You got that Wilson?"

Wilson is still in shock at his request. "Yes Captain" he says nervously, knowing he would have to kill him and the remains of the crew on the ship. He knows it's a last resort, but Drake wouldn't order him to do this without a good reason.

"Good" he says with a smile, "hopefully it won't come to that, Drake out." The vid link goes off and Wilson looks at the crew, and they all look worried.

"Don't worry too much, Drake will sort this son of a bitch out, you'll see." He smiles and the others force a smile back.

On the bridge of the Deep Star Drake and his team stand in a group, and Drake sees Clark near a console, and he goes over to him. "Clark you're part of the engineering crew, do you think you could get the ships internal sensors on line?"

"No problem sir, I'll have them up and running in a jiffy Captain." Drake thanks him and walks away. Denver and Grant follow him as he looks at the main viewer.

"Have you devised a plan sir?" Grant asks as she stands beside him.

"If we can get the sensors on line, then maybe, just maybe we can find this alien's lair and track it's movements around the ship."

"Nice one Captain" Denver adds. "When we know where it is we can trap it."

"Oh yes" he says smiling, "then we can drive it to one of the airlocks and jettison the son of a bitch out into the cold vacuum of space."

"How do we drive it to one of the airlocks though sir?" he looks at Drake. "This creature seems to be very intelligent, and knows its way around the ship."

Drake smiles at them both, then they walk to the others. "We'll use bait" he says, a big grin on his face.

Grant looks at Drake, slightly worried. "Bait sir?" she says nervously, "what kind of bait do you have in mind Captain?"

Drake looks at her, smiling a lot. "Me" he says and they all look stunned.

"No Captain" Denver says out loud, "I can't allow that sir. We need your expertise and cunning to get us out of here sir." he now looks very worried.

"Don't worry, Denver, that alien won't get near me" he looks at them all, "trust me I know what I'm doing." The two of them know it's pointless to argue with Drake because they won't win.

While all this has been going on, Clark has been working on the internal sensors, and he has got them working. "Captain all sensors on line and operational."

Good work Clark. Bring the ships internal structure up on the main viewer" he turns to the viewer. "Let's see who is showing up."

The viewer shows the entire ships full structure and all the decks and rooms throughout the ship. They can see the crew down in engineering and themselves on the bridge as red dots. They all look at the screen and check every inch of the viewer for any other red dot or dots.

They all scan the structure then Finch spots something. "Cap, look there" he says pointing to another red dot. They all see the red dot is moving through the lower cargo bays at the rear of the ship.

"That has to be the alien" Drake says to them, "and it's heading for the engineering room, and Knox and his team." They all watch as the red dot moves erratically through the cargo bays.

"It's heading right for Knox" Henson says worried now.

"Denver, get onto Knox and tell him the alien is on its way to them."

"Right sir, I'm on it." Denver opens a link to the engineering room, but they can't hear them, because they are busy fixing one of the faulty power generators and it's making a lot of noise. He tries 4 times to get through then looks at Drake. "I can't get through to them sir. Either the engine room comms are down or they are making too much noise to hear us."

Ah shit" Drake says out loud, "patch the sensors throughout the ship so we can see where the alien is at all times. We'll have to get down there and quick."

"All sensors patched in sir" Clark says as he gets the sensors up all through the ship.

"Come on you lot, let's get down there before that alien does." Drake grabs his laser gun, as do the rest of them, and they get in the lift.

In the engine room Knox and his team are unaware the alien is closing in on them. Knox, Phillips, Travis and Black are working on the generator, while Hedges is stood at the generators main control console, checking the power as the crew switch each section back on.

Suddenly from behind them the alien appears, and Travis sees it. "The alien" he shouts and they all look round, "watch out Hedges" he says trying to warn him.

They all look at this strange creature, and Hedges looks on it in awe, his mouth wide open. They all get a good look at the alien as it stands in the doorway. It's a huge creature, about 8ft tall and has a muscular body with 4 arms with large hands with razor sharp claws on them. It has 2 large muscular legs with large claws for balance, and then they all look at its head.

The head is large and round and looks like an enormous eye, tapering off at the back to a small round object which the neck is attached to, and behind the round object there is another small object. This has 6 small tubes attached to it. The crew look at the face and they see it has one rectangular slit with a small blue eye in the centre, and below it they see the mouth. The mouth is a larger rectangular shape with a set of razor sharp metal teeth top and bottom. The face has extended veins all over it and 4 tubes link the face to the neck area of the head. It's a very strange creature to these people, but Knox and his team soon stop looking at the face and concentrate on the danger at hand.

They are all amazed to see the alien, but in the blink of an eye it grabs Hedges, and he is picked up like a rag doll and the alien runs off down the corridor as Hedges screams in pain.

Knox and his crew run to the door, but when they get there, the alien is gone. "Bloody hell, did you see that bloody ugly looking thing?" Knox says out loud, and they look at him.

"Yeah" they all reply. They hear a loud scream from the alien's direction, and they look at each other. They stand there, debating whether to follow it or not, then Drake and his team come down the corridor from the opposite direction, and they see the engineers stood in the doorway.

"Captain, are we glad to see you" Knox says, still shaking from the alien's attack.

"What's going on here Knox? I thought you where repairing the generator."

"The alien just grabbed Hedges and took him off down there" and he points to where the alien ran.

"Ah shit, not Hedges now." He sighs as he looks at Knox. "Did you get a look at it Knox?"

"We sure did sir" he says taking a deep breath. "It's a bloody ugly looking creature sir" and he gives them a full description and Drake looks amazed.

"Well the good news is that we now have the sensors on line all over the ship, thanks to Clark here, and we now know where its lair is.

"Where is it sir?" Henson asks him, and he looks at her and grins.

"It's hiding in the lower cargo bays and now all we have to do is find it and lure it into an airlock. Once in we'll jettison it out into space and kill the son of a bitch."

"Have you decided how we are going to do that sir?" Henson asks him.

"I'm going to be the bait and all of you are the trackers. We have to work as a team, or this thing will pick us off one by one." They all know this won't be easy, and the alien is fast and knows its way round the ship, but they have the sensors on their side to track its movements.

"As far as we know this is the only alien on board, so the sooner we get it off the ship, the better and we can get this ship back to Earth and claim our salvage. "

"Just one thing bothers me sir" Black says puzzled, "if you're the bait, doesn't that mean you will have to be in the airlock too?"

"That's right Black" he says then he pats him on the shoulder, "don't worry I have a plan." Drake goes into the engine room and they all follow him. He looks round the room and Knox goes over to him. "Knox, how's it going with the engines?"

"Almost done sir, the engines will be up and running in 20 minutes."

Drake looks at Knox. "Good, carry on." Knox looks at Drake with a bewildered look on his face as he was expecting Drake to give him a lecture. Drake goes to the main viewer and stands there running his plan through his mind of how they are going to lure the alien to the airlock. He turns to his crew. "Can I have your attention please" he says commandingly and they all stop talking and look at him. "Thank you" he pauses, "now this alien has gone through the entire crew of the Deep Star, so it must have taken their bodies down to the lower cargo bays to feast on. Now we are going to find those bodies and line the corridor to the nearest airlock, where I'll be waiting, all suited up."

The crew listen to what he is saying because his life will depend on them knowing what to do, and no one wants to be the one who let their Captain down. Drake walks over to the Captains chair and sits down.

"Now, I will attach a rope to my suit so when the airlock is opened by Knox, I won't be jettisoned out too far, and I can pull myself back to the Deep Star." He looks at his stunned crew, especially Knox. "Any questions?"

The crew all look at him and all of them know this plan is suicide but it's got to work. Phillips walks over to him. "I have a question Captain."

"What is it Phillips?"

"We have to line the corridor with the remains of the Deep Star crew, right?"

"Right" Drake says to him as he looks at his nervous looking face.

"What will the alien be doing while we are stealing its food supply?"

"Hopefully it will be distracted by a couple of you who will be roaming the corridors banging anything metal you can find to make a noise, then over the com I'll tell Knox to lead it to the airlock's corridor, where it will find its food supply. In the mean time the rest of you will be waiting for it to pass the door and you will lose your laser guns to drive it to me in the airlock. You will all have your suits on too, just incase something goes wrong, but don't worry." He looks over to Clark. "Once it's in the airlock with me, open the outer doors immediately, and the rest of you should grab something to hold on at that point too." He looks at his brave crew. "Just remember, don't hit the alien with your laser fire, I just want you to drive it to me, Ok?"

"Yes Captain" they all say at the same time.

"Good, let's get ready then." The crews go back and find their Astro suits and get into them. When everyone is suited up they all go down to the lower cargo bays and search for the crew's remains.

They soon find them dotted around the cargo bays, so they gather all the arms, legs and torso remains they can find and they take them to the corridor leading to the airlock.

While some of the crew where gathering the body parts, the rest of them where keeping a look out for the alien. They lay the remains down the corridor at intervals then they all go into the nearest room to check the sensors to see where the alien is.

Clark runs a ship wide scan and the alien's red dot appears two decks up. "Captain I've found our alien, its two decks up and moving this way."

"I think it knows we stole its food." He looks at his nervous crew. "Ok this is it, grab your noise makers and start making a noise. I'll go and stand in the airlock and Knox you go and stand by the airlock control panel and wait for my command."

"On my way Captain" Knox replies. The rest of them get their laser guns and wait behind the door till the alien passes them.

They all get to their positions and Drake waits in the airlock. Knox is at the airlock control panel and the ones with metal objects start banging them to create a noise to attract the alien.

The alien hears the noise and heads towards it. It doesn't take long for the alien to reach the corridor and there it sees the body remains, and it lets out a very loud roar, and this alerts the crew. The laser guns are armed and the crews making the noise stop and get their guns too.

The alien walks slowly down the corridor gathering its food and the alien doesn't see any of the crew who are hidden. When it passes them they come out and start firing their lasers at the deck and the alien turns to them and lets out a loud roar.

The crew keep firing close to the alien's feet and this makes the creature back away, and it walks backwards along the corridor towards the airlock.

The alien reaches the airlock and walks in, and then it spots Drake near the outer doors. The alien walks over to Drake and outside the airlock Knox sees it getting closer to his Captain so he closes the door.

The alien turns to see the doors closing and tries to run out but it slams into the closed doors. "Now Knox, open the outer doors." Knox opens the outer doors and there is a short hiss, and both of them are jettisoned into space.

The crew rush to the airlock and look out and they see Drake and the alien in outer space, then Drake's safety rope reaches its end, and Drake stops but the alien carries on.

Drake looks back at the airlock and he can see his crew beckoning him to pull himself back to the ship. He grabs the rope and slowly starts to pull himself back, and a minute later he is back in the airlock and Knox closes the outer doors.

Drake looks out the airlock window and he can see the alien floating away, and motionless. He knows it's dead, so he turns to his crew and puts his thumb up to let them know and they cheer. Knox opens the inner doors and the crew cheer and shake Drake's hand.

"Well done Captain" Denver says congratulating him with a hearty handshake.

"Thank you Denver, that means a lot to me." The rest of the crew shake his hand and when they have finished he sits in the Captains chair. "Ok let's get this baby home and claim our well earned salvage." He opens the intercom to the Orion. "Orion this is Drake, come in."

"Captain" Wilson says cheerfully. "It's nice to hear your voice again sir. Is everything Ok over there sir?"

"It sure is Wilson. We jettisoned the alien out of an airlock and all is well. We did lose Hedges though, and I have decided that his share of the salvage will go to his wife and family."

"That's a nice sentiment sir" Wilson says and Drake knows he is choking up because Hedges was a good friend of his.

"It was the right thing to do and he was part of the crew to us all too." Drake pauses, "the crew are returning to the Orion and Knox and I are staying on the Deep Star to bring her back home, Drake out" and he turns the comm link off.

Drake looks at his crew and they all leave the bridge and go back to the Orion. Wilson informs Drake when they are all back on board and Lucas separates the two ships, and they power up and head back to Earth.

The two ships jump into hyperspace and about a day goes past and the two ships come out close to Mars, and the Earth satellites pick them up.

On Harbour 1 Robson is informed that the Deep Star and the Orion are back, so he opens a vid link to the Deep Star, because he knows Drake will be on board.

Drake and Knox are on the bridge looking at Mars when the vid link comes on. "Drake this is Robson, do you hear me?"

"Yeah Robson, I hear you." He looks at Knox, a grin on his face.

"Glad to see you got the Deep Star back in one piece. If you can dock her in Alpha port, I'll meet you all there."

"Ok, Alpha port it is." Drake turns the vid link off and looks at Knox. "He has no idea what we went through to get this ship here eh?"

"No sir, he doesn't."

"Let's get this ship back home so it can end its mission." Drake and Knox take the Deep Star back home to be stripped as salvage and her parts can be used on other ships.

On Harbour 1 Robson has planned a welcome back for Drake and his crew and the tele satellites are all aimed at the Deep Star's flight path so the whole world can see her come home.

The Tv networks are all ready to show the ship coming to port, and people watch anxiously, waiting for their first glimpse of the Deep Star.

Drake guides the ship past Mars and as they approach the moon, the Tv satellites pick them up and pictures are beamed around the world, and people everywhere stop what they are doing and watch.

Drake is on the bridge with Knox and he has been running Robson's message through his mind and he knows he missed something. "Got it" he says suddenly and Knox is surprised.

"Got what sir" he asks puzzled.

"Robson wants the Deep Star docked at the Alpha port" he says looking at Knox, "you know what that means don't you Knox?"

"Not a clue sir, what exactly does it mean sir?"

"It means they are going to rebuild her and not destroy her for parts." Knox is still puzzled then it clicks.

"Does that mean we don't get our salvage Captain?"

"Good question, I'll ask him." Drake opens a link to Robson. "Robson this is Drake, are you there?"

"Right here Drake, what's on your mind?"

"Are you skipping out on paying us the salvage for bringing this ship back" he says and Robson knows his tone of voice means that he wouldn't be happy about that.

"No Drake, you and your crew will still get your salvage but this ship is part of our history and we want the ship restored for the brave crew." He pauses and Drake and Knox look at each other. "Are any of the crew still on board by the way."

"No, there were no crew members alive Robson. I'll tell you the story when I meet you" he pauses, "oh and dinner is on you."

"Ok Drake, bring her home safely, the world is watching you." The link goes off and Drake looks at Knox, who is smiling.

"Why are you smiling Knox?"

"He said the world is watching us sir, we're hero's to them."

Drake laughs. "You bet we are Knox." The Deep Star enters the Earth's atmosphere and the news channels follow it down and Drake docks the ship in Alpha port. News crews are there to see it dock and they see the damage done by the alien and they are amazed it made it back in one piece.

The Orion lands close by and all the crew disembark and meet up with Drake and Knox. There is a huge crowd there and they part as Robson comes forward to meet Drake. He shakes his hand and hands him the salvage cheque, but Drake just puts it in his pocket.

Drake and his crew answer all questions the crowd has, but none of them mention the alien. Robson takes them to the best restaurant and they find a quiet spot and have a meal.

Drake tells Robson what happened on the Deep Star and he is shocked and he is stuck for words, and the crew all know he understands what they all went through.

Of course nothing about the alien or what happened on the Deep Star is ever mentioned and the ship is fully restored and all the data downloaded off the ship.

Drake and his crew pay a special tribute to all the crew of the Deep Star at a private ceremony then have a long break away from the salvage of ships.

THE END

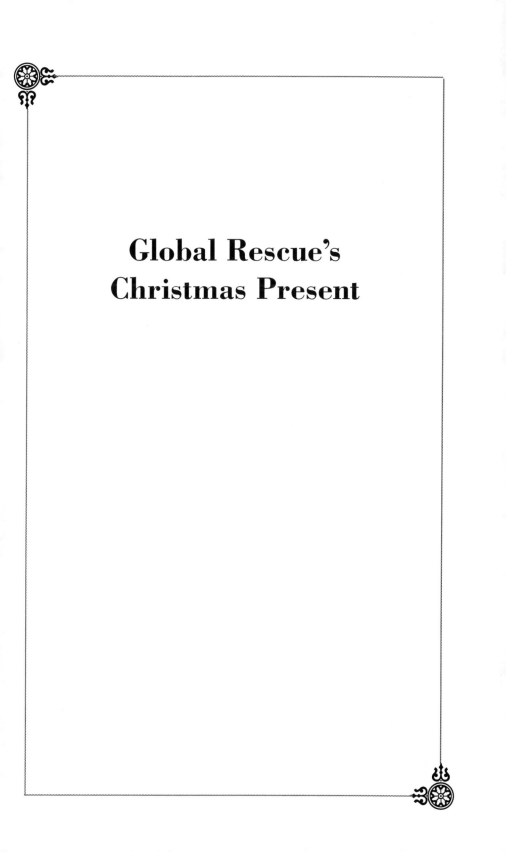

# Global Rescue's
# Christmas Present

# Chapter 1

C hestnut Meadows is a children's orphanage and it holds 30 children, 15 boys and 15 girls. They range in age from 5-10yrs old. The orphanage has been down on its luck for Christmas, but the staff and children are still in high spirits.

The staff of the orphanage have got presents for the children, but with donations being few and far between, they could only afford one present for each child.

The children love Global Rescue and always watch their rescue's on the television when they go on a rescue mission.

Global Rescue have just returned from a mission, a huge fire at a chemical plant, and all the children watched the rescue on the Tv as it was broadcast live. The staff always watch too, and they know the children love this rescue service, and most of all they love them because Global Rescue's base is only 10 miles away from their orphanage.

The children watch the news report on the Tv about the rescue and one boy in particular watches intensely to the report. Global Rescue are his hero's, and he loves to watch them out on a rescue. He always hopes that they will take the crane/ladder truck, as this is his favourite.

The night staff got the children to write their letters to Santa, as they do every year at this time, and the children sit at the tables and write down what they would like the most for Christmas. The next morning the day shift comes in and they get all the children up for breakfast. The children come down and sit at the tables and the head person, Wendy, gets their attention.

"Children, could I have your attention please? Now I hope you have all written your letters to Santa." She looks round the room at them all and they all hold up their letters. "Good. Now the staff will collect them, and then we can post them off striaght away."

The staff collect all the children's letters and the children are all happy and full of smiles. The day staff, Malc, Julie, Jerry, Helen, Sonia, John, Joanne and Brian put all their letters in a special envelope and the children watch as they do, and the staff look at them all, smiles on their faces with excitement.

The children play with toys and games while outside the snow is falling and already it's getting deep around the orphanage.

The dining room/play area has been decorated for Christmas by the staff and children, and it looks so festive. There is tinsel and holly around the pictures and mantle-piece and in the far corner the tree stands fully decorated in glittering baubles and tinsel and lots of lights.

The children always look forward to Christmas and always wake early on Christmas day, eager to see what Santa has brought them.

Wendy has been looking at their letters and then she spots the one from James, the 6yr old boy who was watching the news report with intent.

She gathers the staff. "Look at this" she says, holding the letter. "This is the letter from little James to Santa."

"Aww" the women sigh and the others look at them, smiling.

"Wait till you hear what he has asked Santa for" she says. "Let's go in the staff room." All the staff go to their staff room and Wendy reads the letter to them all.

Dear Santa

Please could you find me a mummy and daddy for Christmas and I hope they have a little brother or sister too.

Could you please look after all the people at Global Rescue and keep them safe when they are out on a rescue because all of us here at the orphanage think they are very brave people and they are our hero's.

    Thank you Santa
        Love from James aged 6yrs.

P.S My favourite is the crane/ladder truck.

The staff look at Wendy, a tear or two in their eyes. "Isn't that nice of James?" Malc says looking at the others.

"That is a really nice letter, isn't it?" Julie says, almost crying.

Wendy looks at her staff. "It sure is, Julie" she says, then a thought come to her. "I have a great idea" she says sitting down at her desk.

"What is it?" Jerry enquires.

"Why don't we see if they would come and visit the children here at the orphanage. The children would love that."

"That's a brilliant idea, Wendy." Jerry looks round at the rest of the staff and they look at him. "Do you think they would come though? They are very busy people."

"I'm not sure Jerry, but it wouldn't hurt to ask. I know they are busy people, but just think what it would mean to the children if they did come."

All the staff look at Wendy for answers, then Jerry speaks out. "How do we call them?"

"Er that's a thought Jerry" Wendy says. "We could use our C.B radio set and hope they would pick it up, or we could go to their base, it's not far away from here."

Malc steps forward. "I'll go" he says and then Helen comes forward aswell.

"Me too, Wendy" she says happily. Wendy looks at them both with a puzzled face.

"Should you just turn up though? I mean they could be away or relaxing after their last rescue.

"No harm in trying, Wendy. There will be someone at the base anyway, so I say let's give it a go."

"Alright Malc, you and Helen go and see if they will come, and we'll all stay here and hope you're in luck." Malc and Helen leave, and they make sure none of the children see them leave.

# Chapter 2

The countryside looks so nice with the covering of snow and the roads are passable, so Helen and Malc head off to Global Rescue's base, but they take it easy on the snow covered roads.

They arrive at the base and pull up infront of the huge main gates. These huge metal gates stand 15ft high and 20tf wide and Malc stops their car to one side of the gates. They both look at the gates, then Helen spots the intercom on one of the huge brick pillars holding the gates.

Malc gets out of the car and goes over to the intercom, and he sees a button with call on it, so he presses it. "Hello" he says, "is there anyone there?"

There is no reply striaght away then a friendly voice answers. "Hello, my name is Penny, how can I help you?"

"My name is Malc, from the local children's orphanage, and I was wondering if I could speak to the person in charge."

"Please wait a moment, and I'll see if he is available." Malc waits and Helen gets out of the car and stands with him.

"What's happening?" she asks Malc. He looks at her.

"I'm just waiting to speak to the person in charge. The lady said she was going to see if he's available."

"Oh" Helen replies and they stand there, in the snow. A few minutes pass and they think no one is going to reply then Helen sees someone walking up the long driveway towards them.

Dave gets to the gate and smiles at Helen and Malc, and he opens the gates and greets them.

"Hello there" he says shaking their hands, "I'm Dave, the head person at the base, how may I help you?"

Malc and Helen look at him. "Sorry to bother you sir, but we are from the orphanage, Chestnut Meadows, 10 miles up this road, and we have come to ask you a special favour."

Dave looks at them, shivering in the cold weather, and he smiles. "How can we at Global Rescue help you, oh and please call me Dave." He smiles at them both again.

"Well Dave we have come to show you a letter one of our children wrote last night, and we thought you should read it." Malc hands Dave the letter, and as the snow falls slowly around them, Dave reads the letter.

"Very nice letter" he says, still smiling, "I'll see what we can do, but I can't promise, but please keep this a secret, just in case we can't make it, Ok?"

"That's no problem Dave, the children don't even know we are here, and thank you for seeing us." He shakes Dave's hand. "I know the children would be over the moon if you could come, but we know you are very busy people, but thanks again for seeing us."

Malc and Helen walk back to their car and get in, and Dave walks over to them, and Helen opens her window. "A merry Christmas to you and all at the orphanage" he says smiling then he bends down and looks at them both, "and I have just come to my decision" he looks at them and they look puzzled. "Look out for us on Christmas morning, we'll be there." Malc and Helen look at Dave, smiles beaming across their faces, and they can't wait to get back and tell the other staff.

"Oh thank you Dave, thank you from the bottom of our hearts, and the children's hearts too. They will be so surprised when you turn up."

"Don't forget, say nothing to the children" Dave says to the two of them and they promise him. Dave starts to walk away to let them get back and tell the staff, then a thought enters his mind and he goes back to the car. "I forgot to ask, how many children do you care for?"

"We have 15 boys and 15 girls Dave, ranging in age from 5-10yrs old." Helen smiles at Dave because she is so happy the children are going to meet their hero's.

"Good" he says, "see you all on Christmas day. Have a safe journey back won't you?"

"We will Dave," Helen replies. "One more thing Dave, how will we know when you are there?" She looks at Dave.

"Oh you'll know, believe me." He says grinning at them both. "Merry Christmas." He shakes their hands. Dave stands back and they pull out of the drive and head back to the orphanage.

Back at the orphanage the children are still playing games, totally unaware that Malc and Helen have been missing for over 2 hours. The staff watch and join in their games, awaiting their return.

Wendy is sat in the office when she sees the headlights of the car as they pull up outside the office. She goes to the other staff and discreetly calls them into the office. They all go into the office just as Malc and Helen walk in, from the outside door.

"So did you get to speak to anyone?" Wendy asks them.

"Oh yes, we certainly did" Malc says smiling. "We spoke to the head person, a man called Dave. He came to the main gates to meet us in person and we chatted. A very nice and polite man he was too."

Wendy looks at them both. "What did he say?"

Helen smiles and the others are hopeful. "At first he said he would see what they could do, but just as we were leaving he said they would come."

"Oh that's great news. The children will be so surprised." She looks at her staff, and they are all smiling too. Julie goes over to Malc and looks at him as the message has not yet sunk in for her.

"They're really going to come?" she asks Malc.

"Oh yes Julie, Global Rescue are coming here on Christmas day." He smiles at her and all the staff are in very high spirits now. "I don't know about you lot, but I can't wait, let alone the children."

That night the children sit down to their tea in the dining part of the room, and then James stands up, and the staff are puzzled.

"Miss Wendy" he says in a low voice, "did you post our letters to Santa?" the children look at her, smiles on their faces.

"Yes we did, James. Santa is probably reading them right now."

"Thank you Miss Wendy" he says and sits down. The children are really excited now, and they carry on eating their meal.

# Chapter 3

On the base, Dave has gathered all his team together in the main command centre and they stand their looking puzzled.

"This morning we had a visit from the local orphanage, and I was handed a letter from one of the children there. I'll read it out to you." Dave reads the letter out to them all, and at the end he looks round the command centre at his loyal team, and most of them have a tear in their eyes.

One of them walks upto Dave. "Are we going Dave?" Lesley asks him, wiping a small tear from her eye. "It would be nice to see the children at the orphanage, and it would make their day and ours too . . . right?" she says looking round at all the others.

"Right" they all reply.

"Yes Lesley, we are going. We'll take some of the rescue vehicles with us too, and to make it even more special for them, I thought we could bring them back here for a party, a big meal, games and lots of presents too."

Harry steps forward. "What a brilliant idea, Dave, they'll love that and what a great surprise. I can't wait to see the look on their faces.

"Me too, Harry." Dave looks round the room at his eager team. "Now we need to get presents for 30 children, 15 for the boys and 15 for the girls. They range in age from 5-10yrs old." He looks at them. "Any volunteers?"

Everyone's hand goes up and Dave feels so proud of his team, so he picks out 10 of them to get the presents. The rest will have the great job of re-decorating the living area with a new bigger tree and all decorations on it, and they will also hang lots of trimmings and balloons around the room.

Some will help to cook the meals and set up a buffet for when the children arrive. The place becomes a hive of activity as there are only 4 days left till Christmas day, so everyone works hard.

The meals are to be prepared while some of the crews are at the orphanage, picking up the children. Dave sets out a plan so that everyone will do something to help with the festivities, and no one will be left out.

Christmas Eve arrives, the presents have been bought and wrapped and the meals are all ready to be cooked. The living area has been decorated out like an indoor winter wonderland, and the masses of light twinkle all around the room, and the huge 12ft Christmas tree has lots of baubles and lights on it, and the lights twinkle on and off, making the room look very cosy.

Outside the snow is still falling gently and Dave and some of the vehicle crews are out preparing the vehicles to be used ready for tomorrow. Dave wants one of the snow crawlers to go, and this can be used to bring the children and staff back to the base. Dave is also taking the crane/ladder truck because in his letter, James said this was his favourite.

They are going to take one of the fire tower trucks, 2 road cruisers and 2 super ambulance buses. Dave gets the crews to put a warm jacket for each child in the snow crawler, and he secretly got the sizes of every child and the staff from Wendy yesterday over the phone, and even the other staff don't know about this, as they have jackets for them too, all with their logo on them.

The crews work into the late hours getting the vehicles ready for the big day, and when they have finished they go to bed for a good sleep. They plan to leave the base around 9am so they can get to the orphanage for when the children are up and in their dining room for breakfast.

The next morning Dave and his crews are ready to go, and the rest of the base is a hive of activity as the meals are being prepared to be cooked and everyone is in high spirits waiting for the children to arrive.

Dave and the crews get in their vehicles, the engines roar into life, and they set off on their way through the deep snow.

At the orphanage all the children are up and in the dining room eating their breakfasts and they are all happy and jolly because it's Christmas day. The staff watch them and they sit there knowing what is going to happen shortly, and smile to themselves.

After their breakfasts the children sit around the tree and open their presents. The children rip the wrapping off their presents and paper flies in all directions, but they clear up their mess afterwards.

James is over the moon with his present, because he got a truck that looks a lot like the crane/ladder truck of Global Rescue. The staff gather near the tree while the children play with their toys.

"Just look at the look on James' face, he is so thrilled with his toy" Wendy says looking at her staff.

"He loves it, doesn't he?" Malc says looking at James.

"Yes he does" Wendy says softly, "just imagine the look on his face when Global Rescue get here."

"Ooh, that's what I'm looking forward to. The children are going to be so surprised." Sonia looks at the children then she looks at the other staff.

"They should be here soon, so don't let on, none of you Ok?" Wendy looks out the window, and the staff go and join in with the children as they play. They play and chat with the children, and then they all hear a loud air horn.

The children stop playing and look at the staff, then at each other. The staff shrug their shoulders, pretending they don't know what it was. Then there is another blast of the air horn and the children look at the staff, and they smile at them and point to the window.

The children get up excitedly and run to the windows to look out. They all see lots of bright lights coming up the driveway, then through the snow fall they see the vehicles.

James sees the crane/ladder truck at the front. "It's Global Rescue" he says jumping up and down, and some of the others are doing the same, "have they come to see us Miss Wendy?"

The staff go to the window and look out as the mighty vehicles come up the driveway. "Yes they have James." she says looking at their bright glowing faces and they all look out the windows. "They have come to see you all, children" she says smiling at them all, "merry Christmas children."

They all watch as the vehicles pull up outside the orphanage and Wendy looks at the children. "Who wants to go and meet them then?" she is almost deafened by the shouts of "me" as they all say it at the same time. "Come on then, let's go meet them."

The children are very eager to get outside and they wait for the staff to take them out. They all go out and stand on the porch and they look at the huge rescue vehicles. James doesn't take his eyes off the crane/ladder truck then he sees Dave come round the front of the truck.

The staff have held the other children back for one reason, and as James recognises Dave he runs over to him and Dave sees him running towards him so he stops. James puts his arms round Dave's legs and hugs him, and Dave looks down at him. James looks up, a beaming smile on his face.

"Hello there little sir, I guess you are James?"

James is very surprised he knows his name. "Yes sir, I am." James lets go of Dave, and he kneels down infront of him.

"Nice to meet you James, my name is Dave." James is speechless. "So James, Santa has told me about your letter, and it was so heart warming, we just had to come and see you all."

"Thank you sir" he says in a soft voice, "it's so nice to meet you." James shakes Dave's hand.

"It's our pleasure, James" Dave walks him over to the crane/ladder truck and James' eyes light up as he stands next to the massive truck. Dave looks at him. "I hear this is your favourite vehicle, James."

"Yes sir, it is. I think it's fantastic." James looks at the truck and Dave looks round and sees his crews showing the other vehicles to the other children and chatting with them and the staff.

A few of the children come over to them and Dave looks at their eager faces. "Come on then, let's go on board eh?" the children cheer and Dave takes them into the cab of the crane/ladder truck, and James sits in the driver's seat, and for him it's the best present he has ever had.

The staff and other children go on all the vehicles and look around, and enjoy themselves. The crews explain anything they want to know and when they have all had a good look around they all go back into the orphanage. James shows Dave his Christmas present and he looks at Dave and Dave has a good look at the truck.

"This looks like our crane/ladder truck doesn't it James?"

"Yes sir, that's why I love it."

"You can't keep calling me sir, James, please call me Dave Ok."

"Ok Dave" James says as he puts his truck down near the tree. The staff and children talk for a long time to all the Global Rescue crews and after a short while, the staff make them a nice warm drink. Well time passes and Dave decides it's time to go and he stands up. A little girl goes over to him

"You're not going are you Dave?" she looks up at Dave a sad look on her face.

Dave kneels and looks at her. "We have to sweetheart" he says looking at her, "but you are all coming back with us to our base, where we have some special surprises for you all." Melony looks at Dave then she puts her arms round him and kisses him on the cheek.

James was not far away and heard what Dave said so he goes over to them. "Are we really going to your base, Dave?"

"You sure are James, all of you in fact even the staff are coming too."

The staff all look at Dave, surprised, and they are now in high spirits, just like the children. Everyone leaves the orphanage and they get on the vehicles. James, Melony and a couple of the other children go on the crane/ladder truck while the rest and the staff go on the snow crawler.

# Chapter 4

B ack at the base the rest of the Global Rescue teams are preparing for the children and staff's arrival. The command centre receives a call from Dave to tell them they are on their way, and the word goes out around the base and everyone is so excited that they are going to entertain the children and staff.

The vehicles plough through the snow on their way back to the base, and on the snow crawler the children and staff are singing Christmas carols, joined by the Global crew. On the crane/ladder truck the children are looking at the big screens and pictures of Christmas, but James is sat in the co-driver's seat, and thoroughly loving it.

They soon reach the base and pull up outside the main building, and the engines are turned off and the children look around the massive open area of the base and in the distance they can see the big jets and super carriers, all covered in snow, then they all go into the living area of the base.

The children look all around the wonderfully decorated place, and the other crew members greet them as they come in. The children and staff are all given a hat as they enter, and the children are smiling happily. They spot the big 12ft tree at the far end of the room, and all the trimmings and lights around it.

The dining tables have been laid out with decorations and a big cracker for each child and staff member and down the centre of the table are candles, all lit and giving off a cosy flickering.

They are all offered a mince pie, if they want one, and the staff are given a drink of their choice. In the background, Christmas songs are playing low, and everyone is in high spirits.

The children go over to the tree and under it they see lots and lots of presents and after a good look around Dave comes upto them.

"Could all the staff and children please be seated, we are about to serve you all a meal, then afterwards we can all play games." The children cheer and sit down at the table.

The crews bring in their meals, and what a meal it is too. They all tuck in and while this is going on, Dave and some of his crew go and set the games up. They have board games and various other things they can all do.

The children and staff finish their meals and sit down till it has settled, then Dave announces its fun time. They all pick something to do and even the Global Rescue crews join in the fun and activities.

The children pick their games, and they have a choice from Operation, Hungry Hippo's, Mouse trap and others and there is a Spyrograph set for the children to draw some pretty patterns, and some of them do them for the people of Global Rescue. Others play pin the tail on the donkey and musical chairs, and the staff and the crews all join in.

Dave gets Lesley in a corner, out the way of the children's hearing range because he needs to ask her a special question.

"Lesley, is the special present for James ready yet?" He looks at her and she smiles back at him.

"It sure is Dave. Shall I bring it in now?"

"No" he says softly, "take it to the command centre and put it on a table in the middle of the room, and cover it up please, we all want to see his face when he uncovers it." Dave looks at Lesley, a grin on his face, and she realises why now.

"Leave it to me Dave" she starts to walk away then turns round to him, "he's going to love his present, I'm sure of that, Dave."

The children are having lots of fun playing games and eating more food from the buffet laid out by the Global crew. Dave spots Harry, and calls him over.

"Harry, I'm off to dress up as Santa for the present giving, so give me 5 minutes then get everyone around the tree, Ok."

"Right" he says then goes off. Dave leaves the room and goes to his quarters and puts on the Santa suit, and when he's ready he goes back to the main living room. Harry looks at his watch and sees the 5 minutes are up.

"Can I have your attention please children and staff, could everyone please gather round the tree, there is someone here to see you all." The children look surprised and start clapping in excitement. They all go to the tree and their staff follow them, and everyone sits down on the floor. The children look all around, waiting for the special someone to come, and then Dave comes in the room, and the children cheer and clap as they see Santa.

"Ho! Ho! Ho!" he says in a deep and loud voice, and he looks at the children. "Hello to you all" Dave says as he goes over to them and they are so excited. "Now let's see who has a present under this magnificent tree shall we?" He looks at the children and they all shout out "Yeah" at the same time.

Dave starts shouting their names out, and they go up and collect their present, then go sit down and open what they got. Dave does this for everyone, including his crews. The children love their presents and they thank Santa for them, and none of them still have no idea it's Dave.

Dave leaves the room because he wants the children to think the real Santa gave them their presents, so he leaves quietly, and goes to take the suit off then he goes back to the main living room. He sees the children having a sing song with his crews as he comes in.

"Ooh, what did I miss here?" he says, pretending he doesn't know. In the background, silent night plays low.

Little Melony comes running over to him, a huge smile on her face. "Dave you missed Santa" she says holding his hand.

"Santa?" he says, still pretending, "awe, I would have liked to have seen Santa too." He looks at Melony, and she is still smiling at him.

James comes over to them and tugs at Dave's jumper. "What's up, James?" he says as he kneels down to him.

"Dave, you have a present under the tree too." James points to the tree and all around the room the Global crews and the children's staff all play along with Dave on this.

"I do?" he says looking at James and Melony.

"Yes you do, Dave" Melony says in such a lovely soft voice, and they all go over to the tree. James picks the present up and hands it to Dave. Dave opens it and it's a new watch, and he looks at the two children and puts his arms around them and they hug him.

The Global crews are almost in tears at this wonderful sight, and they all know it's all down to Dave, and the gift he has given these children. Dave looks at everyone and stands up.

"Come on then, let's all of us have a sing song." The children cheer then gather round him and they all have a good sing song. Lesley comes over to Dave and tells him the special present is ready. Dave stands and looks at the children.

"Ok children, let's go to the command centre" he says and the children are excited and one asks him why. "I have a special present for someone here, and it's in the command centre, so let's go."

Everyone goes to the command centre and the children and the staff look all around at the many displays and big screens, and the crews guide them into the room and in the middle there is a table, with something covered up. Dave gets the children to stand near the table. Dave stands on the opposite side of the table and all the children look at him.

"This special present is for one child here" and they all look very surprised at him, "and this one is for the child who wrote a letter to Santa, and asked Santa that he would like to meet us." All the children look at each other then they all look at James.

"That was you, James." Melony says to James, and she hugs him.

James is surprised and looks at Dave. "Me" he says and Dave nods his head.

"Yes James, you. I got this special present just for you for your heart warming letter." James lifts the cover off the object, and when he sees it his face lights up. The other children look at his present and cheer for him.

The special present is a large model of the crane/ladder truck James loves so much, and it's very detailed. This is a toy for him to play with, and it has a working crane that extends, just like the real one, and the ladder part also works like the real one too. The truck is about 3ft long and was built by several of his crew, especially for James.

Dave looks at James, who has a tear in his eyes. "Merry Christmas, James" he says to him, and James goes round the table to Dave and Dave kneels and James gives him the biggest hug he has ever given to anyone. Everyone says "awe" as he does, and Dave thanks him and the children for a wonderful Christmas day.

Dave has yet another present to give, but this is for the staff, but he doesn't let on yet, he's waiting till they get back to the orphanage.

Well the time comes for them to go back home, to the orphanage, and the children are a little sad, but they know they have to.

Dave drives them all back in the crane/ladder truck and they have a sing song on the way back. The snow is still falling as they go back, and the children and the staff are very happy.

Dave and some of his crew stay at the orphanage till the children go to bed, but none of them go to sleep because they're waiting for Global Rescue to leave.

Down stairs, Dave and his crew are chatting to the staff, and they thank Dave and his crews for the lovely day out.

"It's been a great day for us, and for the children Dave, and we all thank you for taking time out to entertain us." Wendy looks at them all and smiles happily.

"It was our pleasure" he says shaking her hand. "It was nice to have children around the base, and let's face it eh, Christmas is for the children."

"We enjoyed every second of their company, and yours too." Lesley says shaking Wendy's hand. Dave looks at his crew and nods at them, and they know what he's going to do now.

"I have noticed that this place is looking a bit run down and in need of some repairs, so" and he puts his hand into his pocket and pulls out a piece of paper, "this is for your orphanage." He hands Wendy the piece of paper.

She opens it, and it's a cheque for a very large amount of money, and she gasps in shock. "What's this for, Dave?"

"It's to get all your repairs done, and get new blankets, pots, pans or whatever you need."

"That's very kind of you, Dave. We'll get all that done after the holidays, you can be sure of that." The rest of the staff thank them all, and Dave says it's time to go. The staff walk Dave and his crew back to the truck, and they get one last look at this huge vehicle.

"This is one heck of a truck, Dave" Malc says looking at the crane/ladder truck.

"Yeah, she's the pride of our fleet" Dave says patting the side of the truck. Well, time for us to go" and he looks at the staff, "a very merry Christmas to you all and a happy new year."

"And the same to you, all of you. Thanks once again for the special day out. The children will talk about this forever."

They climb back on the truck and Dave starts it up and the truck roars into life, and the children hear it, and all run to the windows. They stand with their noses pressed on the window glass and watch as the mighty truck pulls away and disappears down the drive in the falling snow.

The children get into bed and settle down and they sleep and dream of their day out at Global Rescue's base, and all the fun and games they all played, and the wonderful food and decorations, and each child is soon fast asleep.

The End